# BEST GAY EROTICA 2010

# BEST
# GAY EROTICA
# 2010

*Series Editor*

RICHARD LABONTÉ

*Selected and Introduced by*

BLAIR MASTBAUM

Published in the United States.
Cleis Press Inc., P.O. Box 14697, San Francisco, California 94114.

Printed in the United States.
Cover design: Scott Idleman
Cover photograph: Jack Slomovits/Getty Images
Text design: Frank Wiedemann
Cleis logo art: Juana Alicia
First Edition.
10 9 8 7 6 5 4 3 2 1

ISBN 13: 978-1-57344-374-6

*For Asa…*
*who has found his "best home ever"*
*on Bowen Island.*

# CONTENTS

# FOREWORD

Fifteen years of *Best Gay Erotica*. My, my. Fourteen of those under my stewardship. Who knew we'd be together between the covers for so long, this annual erotica collection and this one-time gay bookseller...or gay-book seller, as it were? I've read (confession: many I skimmed...first pages often tell all) close to four thousand stories over the years, and selected about six hundred for my fourteen judges to review, from Douglas Sadownick in 1997 and Christopher Bram in 1998 to James Lear in 2009 and Blair Mastbaum in 2010. The result: about twenty of the best short stories every year blending sexual intensity and—always my goal—literary craftsmanship.

Back when *BGE* made its debut, nonerotic literary anthologies were a going concern. All this happened in the nineties: David Bergman became editor of Plume's venerable *Men on Men* series after the death of its founding editor, George Stambolian. Brian Bouldrey was compiling the *Best American Gay Fiction* collections for Little, Brown. Faber & Faber released three volumes of *His* (exuberantly subtitled *Brilliant New Fiction by Gay Writers*), edited by Robert Drake and Terry Wolverton. Alyson Books published an anthology almost every year, among them *Certain Voices*, edited by Daryl Pilcher; *Circa 2000*, edited by Drake and Wolverton; and *Not the Only One*, a collection of gay short stories for the young adult crowd. David Leavitt and Mark Mitchell assembled *The Penguin Book of Gay Short Stories*, and Mitchell put together *The Penguin Book of International Gay Writing*. There was even a *Mammoth Book of Gay Short Stories*, edited by Peter Burton for Carroll & Graf. These are but a few collections among many, including a slew of science fiction, mystery, and horror titles, where short gay fiction could be found.

Those were the good old days of queer literary fiction. Now we're lucky if we get one or two such collections a year.

Which is where *BGE* comes in. I take the "erotica" part of the title seriously: porny is good, and that's what this annual anthology hews to. But every year I encourage writers of a literary bent to sex up their stories some, and every year I coax polished prose from writers who honed their horndog skills in the glossy gay mags.

Meanwhile, outlets for erotica have shrunk as well: Mavety Media announced in May 2009 that it was suspending its gay magazines. *Torso*, *Mandate*, *Inches*, *Playguy*, *Honcho*—all gone. (A question for Queer Trivia, should there ever be such a game: which *BGE* judge once worked as an editor for Mavety Media? I'll never tell.) The fiction published in those magazines was often rigidly formulaic and sexually hyperbolic, but *BGE* has featured a few classy tales from their pages. Now that market has vanished, so it's up to collections like this, and others from ever-inventive Cleis Press, to keep cum alive...creatively and with literary flair.

Richard Labonté
Bowen Island, British Columbia

# INTRODUCTION: REALLY, IT'S ALL YOU, AND ALL NATURAL

Blair Mastbaum

Porn has a much more significant place in our lives since the Internet delivered first photos, and now video clips, cams, and chat. It's everywhere, and everyone talks about it. I wonder, though, if this public acceptance and proliferation isn't making it kinda boring. More like...television. (Maybe my friends are a bunch of pervs, but talking about visual porn with them is like talking about where to eat dinner that night—not a big deal in the slightest.)

That's why the written word remains important when it comes to sex. Words bring porn back into the private realm. Words put the erotic back in your mind. You conjure up the images when you're reading, with cues and hints from the author. But really, it's all you.

Think about it. Letters—and words—are symbols and series of symbols, and you're *seeing something* when you read those words. It's incredible, and it's beautiful. (And I always want to find some guy reading Shakespeare on XTube. I think it would be sexy.)

I really don't understand the hesitancy about sexuality. There's nothing dirty about sex. It's as natural as breathing. Our body tells us what makes it happy, sad—or randy. It tells us as we read something or watch something or hear something, or just think of something, that it's erotic, and we respond. Or at least we ought to.

Great sex is narrative unto itself. There's a wordless story—a beginning, a middle, and an end. I'm not talking about those forced stories in seventies porn films. I'm talking about the process—being turned on, randomly, impulsively, or on purpose; initiating the sex, performing it, and finally, if you're lucky I suppose, cumming. It starts on a train, or on a hiking trail, or in a college classroom, and it ends up somewhere smaller, darker perhaps, more private, and weirder, even if it's just behind a grove of trees or in the janitor's closet.

And it also starts on the pages of this collection.

Sex for fun is one of the most obvious aspects of what separates us from most other animals. Okay, yes, bonobos do it—but they can't read.

So read this book. Prove to the bonobos that they have nothing on us. This book is art, really. Sometimes, the sex is secondary. It's the words that are primary.

Blair Mastbaum

# HOLIDAY FROM LOVE

Hank Fenwick

When I think of Erik I think first (and very definitely foremost) of his dick. It was—I hope and trust it still is—a lovely thing, long without being intimidating, sturdy without looking like a club, warmly pink, rising (almost always rising) out of a mop of light-brown curls. It was very much like its owner—well worthy of affection and respect.

The thing I respected most about him was his discipline. It was almost impossible to deflect him from his plans—especially when his plans involved getting an early start at a day's work. Erik is a painter, rather a good one, I think, but at that time he made his living as an illustrator and he created that work on his computer. His weekend days were given over to paint and canvas in a borrowed studio and he didn't like to waste any of the light. Many Sunday mornings I stretched out on the bed, trying to look seductive, watching the sun begin to touch the treetops outside, reaching to catch that bobbing, half-hard truncheon of flesh with my mouth as its owner gathered up his clothes.

I succeeded only once, by changing my tactics. He was stooping, one leg raised as he put on his underpants, and instead of aiming for his dick I lunged for his arse. It surprised him so much he stumbled, I drove my tongue into his crack, and he turned to escape. That was his mistake: his ass was mine, as was his dick. So was the next half hour. I gorged on the shaft then returned to his sweet, musky hole. He'd showered quickly after wakening, and there was a faint smell of soap, a reminiscence of shit, a warmth of sweat as we bucked on the mattress.

He was annoyed, laughing but annoyed with me for distracting him, with himself for being distracted, and that current of annoyance affected the sex. He was usually gentle, almost pedantic in the way he led me along, like an infinitely patient sex therapist. This time the gentleness vanished.

As I buried my face in the curves of his behind he twisted his body so that I was trapped under him and he bore down on my mouth. He had strong thighs, strong glutes, and he raised himself up so that he was sitting on my head, impaling himself on my tongue. I'd lost the advantage, he was in charge, and he made sure I could feel it. I was suffocating in that sexy stink. I drilled my tongue deep into him but I needed to breathe and I couldn't. I tried to pull my head away, just for a minute, to catch some air. He pressed harder, grinding my head into the mattress with his weight. I flailed and he relented, pulling himself back a few inches. He leaned over and grabbed my jaw with one hand, forcing my mouth to open wider.

"Suck my balls," he said. "Gently!" That "gently" had a note of threat to it. And he straddled my neck, dipping first one hairy egg then the other into my open mouth. Then he drew away, moving down the bed until he was between my legs.

Before, when he'd fucked me, he'd taken it gently, licking, stroking, working lube into me until I was all hole, waiting for him. Now he grabbed my thighs, threw my legs up onto his shoulders, and hit me across the buttocks with the flat of his hand fast and hard. I'd barely registered the sting when he did it again, on the other side; then the first, then the second again. I was burning. And that was it for foreplay. He placed the head of his beautiful dick against my sphincter and pushed, not quickly but not slowly either. It was an efficient thrust and god, how I felt it. I started to roar, with pain and also with the shock of pleasure, and he clamped his left hand over my mouth. He was always respectful of the neighbors and it was, after all, still early on a Sunday morning.

Neither of us lasted much longer. It was a fast, fierce, aiming-for-orgasm fuck. I came helplessly, the sperm pushed out of me in short, hard jerks, and he spread the come over my chest and face as he came himself, leaning into me. Then he got up off the bed, put on his clothes, and left for the studio. I stayed in bed a long time cherishing the soreness inside me.

I was never able to repeat the experience. He hadn't been really pleased to lose that half hour. He thought it a failure of self-discipline. He was too generous to blame me, but he guarded himself better against me in the mornings after that. But I regarded myself as a potential bad influence—and what a pleasure that was. All my romantic life I had been the stable one, the one who tried to maintain sanity. Being coupled with someone who did all that stable stuff, and did it so much better than I ever had, was a rest, a relief, an unbelievable indulgence.

Going to bed with him had always been a totally happy experience, sensual and domestic. He may have had a schedule but he had no inhibitions and he took real pleasure in overcoming mine. That may have been why he was taken off guard by my arse attack; rimming had been part of his repertoire, not mine.

* * *

Affection and respect aside, the fact is that we picked each other up on the street. It was in the west eighties, between Columbus Avenue and Amsterdam, and we passed each other, looked, stopped, looked back, and I asked him home with me. I must have been feeling uncharacteristically confident that evening. I don't know how he was feeling but he's told me since that he has a weakness for my body type. He didn't describe it as a weakness; he just said he fancies it. Likes lanky, I suppose.

He's not my type. Usually I go for the tormented, dark, Heathcliff sort—a touch of Montgomery Clift. It's not a healthy taste. He's Danish, with a cheerful Scandinavian face and a purposeful manner. The manner isn't a pose; he usually *has* a purpose. I'm amazed, looking back, that he went home with me that night. Perhaps his schedule said *Get Laid*—and he did.

My place was a sublet in a run-down apartment building in the northern reaches of Central Park West—I'd been lucky finding it through friends. Nowadays it would cost a fortune and even then it was a find. He had an even smaller place on Amsterdam Avenue, just a few blocks away, and he borrowed studio loft space from a friend downtown. He used the studio on weekends and sometimes, very rarely, during the week. He could use it all day if his friend was in the country, but otherwise he guaranteed to be out of there by ten A.M., which was when his friend liked to start work. That's why those early hours were so important to him. After that one successful seduction my bobbing for his dick became a ritual, a gesture without any real intention of consummation, a mutual joke. Sometimes he would wag his half-erection at me to wave good-bye.

Because he was so much not my type there was always an element of surprise in seeing him in bed. I'd look at him and I'd start to laugh. How the hell did this happen? How did it turn into a regular thing? Not only in bed. We'd be sitting opposite each other at one of those tiny New York café tables, having a quick snack (he didn't drink, which for me was another oddity in a partner), and I'd watch him eating and the laughter would begin somewhere near my stomach and then spill out and I'd be laughing, then he'd laugh though he never quite understood what I was laughing about, then I'd get hard just looking at him sitting so close across the table and I'd wonder how I was going to stand up without everyone in the place seeing the growing pyramid in my pants. What could be better than that, laughing and getting a hard-on simultaneously?

He'd have been pleased if everyone in the place had noticed the boner he'd given me. It would have amused him to see me embarrassed, and of course it would have been points to him. But the embarrassment would have been the gratifying thing—he wasn't vain. I whispered to him, once, when he wanted to leave, that I couldn't get up, I needed a minute for my hard-on to wilt. He grinned and got up anyway, moving to the door. I hobbled after him, trying to use the paperback I was carrying as some sort of shield. He stopped, suddenly, so that I bumped into him and that damned erection probed into his backside. He started laughing then and so I did too, though I only found it half funny at the time. I took to carrying a book bag to conceal my crotch.

In bed our sex was a tussle for the top position, a fight I usually let him win. Outside of bed I didn't find it so easy to give in, so our arguments could be edgy. Not that we disagreed about anything substantive; he was, I think, a better person than I am and in some moods I would like to have been more like him. They were more about matters of taste—a disagreement about a painter, a movie, a book. Those aren't insignificant when both your careers are involved in things like that. I've known long-term feuds to spring up from people taking sides over a play or a film.

But at least we were interested in the same things, even if we didn't react to them in the same way. Neither of us had much money but I had contacts that got us into a lot of places and events where Erik didn't have access. I remember one evening we began by going to a reception at the Metropolitan Museum; I can't recall who the painter was but it was someone Erik admired. He drank tonic and I drank the champagne on offer and he explained to me the different things he liked about the work. He liked to explain things to me and sometimes I let him.

Then we went on to a party in the west seventies, where a Danish dancer, a major ballet star and a notoriously handsome man, was the guest of honor. I knew the host, and Erik wanted to meet the dancer; he had been a fan since he was a teenager. We had spent longer at the exhibition than we had intended so I suggested splurging on a taxi across Central Park rather than waiting for a bus. Erik vetoed the taxi, said it would be faster to walk than wait for a bus. *Always assuming*, I thought, *that we don't get mugged on the way*. There'd been a lot of stuff in the papers about robberies in the park. I said something wimpy, like "Do you think we should?" and Erik said, full of purpose, "Of course, why not?" So we set off.

The light had gone—it was nine o'clock on a November night—and I was nervous. But I was also exhilarated. I told myself that Erik was well-built and that I was tall so together we probably looked like a team that shouldn't be messed with. I twitched at every rustle in the bushes but kept up my side of the conversation as gamely as I could, so he wouldn't know I wasn't as confident as he was. I was surprised when we saw the lights and traffic of Central Park West just ahead of us. He had been right, it had been quicker to walk. No bus had passed us on the way.

The party was a success. There was a big buffet and the exercise had made me hungry so I wolfed down chili and salad while I chatted to our host.

"We walked across the park so I'm really famished," I told him, apologizing for my concentration on his food.

"You walked across the park!" he said, gratifyingly horrified.

"Sure," I shrugged. "Why not?"

"You're crazy," he said but there was a hint of envy in his voice. Maybe he fancied Erik but I knew his estimate of me had gone up.

I talked to the host's wife and watched Erik network. The star was looking even more handsome than his pictures, though a little bit worn around those beautiful edges. He and Erik chatted together for a few minutes in Danish—I don't speak Danish but they were both from Denmark so what else would it have been—then Erik came over and said he was ready to leave if I was. We went to say goodnight to the host and he saw us to the door—I think he wanted to find out more about Erik, whose hand was on my backside, guiding me out.

That evening stands out for me, because it was so close to the last. He had been offered a job in San Francisco, a good one, teaching computer graphics, and he had accepted. That was something else we disagreed about: he loved that city. I suppose I could have learned to like it but we weren't a couple and we had never seriously talked about my going with him, or after him. When we got back to my place that night we were both aware that in a few days he would be gone. There was nothing to be sentimental about but it affected the way we touched each other. When I took his shirt off I inhaled the sweat from his armpit.

"I feel like Greta Garbo in *Queen Christina*," I joked. "Saying good-bye to her room."

"I don't remember Garbo smelling anyone's armpit," he said and offered me his other one. I took it. "And you don't look like Garbo."

"No," I said. "But that ballet dancer does!"

"Yes," he said. "He does, a bit." We grinned at each other. We both knew I wasn't jealous but the idea was an interesting one.

"Do you wish you'd brought him back?" I said.

"It's your apartment," he said, pragmatically.

I pushed him back onto the bed.

"Do you wish it was him who was going to fuck you right now?" I challenged.

"Who's going to fuck who?" he said, but we had really already decided. That night it was definitely my turn.

"Don't move," I said, and I started to unbutton his jeans. "And you'll find out."

He watched me as I peeled his fly open and delicately took out his cock. I rolled his foreskin between my fingers. I'm circumcised so that was always another point of interest. Sometimes we'd lie, erection facing erection, and he'd roll his foreskin down and over my glans. Tonight he lay still and I stretched the skin until it was a tube for my tongue. I probed gently, and he stirred a little as I tickled the tip of his prick, I'd never seen him quite so passive.

He loved attention to his balls, his perineum, the shaft of his penis, but tonight I decided to remind him he had an arsehole, finish that rimming he hadn't let me deliver on that triumphant Sunday morning. I trailed my tongue down between his legs, raised his thighs, and circled his pink pucker, slavering saliva round his hole, pushing it in with first my tongue and then my finger. He pushed slowly down, taking the finger farther into him. I pushed my middle finger in after it, and wiggled them. He felt smooth and velvety, pliable, as manipulable as a glove puppet. I looked up at him, through his legs, across his genitals, along his torso, to his face. His eyes were open and he was watching me. We smiled at each other then I pulled my hand away and sniffed my fingers, then reached up and rubbed his mouth. He wrapped his lips around them and I kneeled up and turned him over onto his stomach. He rolled easily with me, letting me do whatever I wanted.

I pulled on a condom and lubed myself up, then I pulled his buttocks apart. He had a magnificent rear, full and round and muscular, and I would have liked to play with it longer, but even more I wanted to be inside him. I eased myself in, trying to feel every centimeter of the way, slowly and with concentration, a diamond miner searching for the great discovery that would make him rich. My prick had never felt so alive, a separate part of me with its own separate knowledge, sending urgent, intense codes to the brain. I could feel the messages traveling along my nerves, making my guts turn over, untranslatable into words my brain could understand. I thrust, spiraling down and in, pausing for a beat, then drawing slowly out. I was dripping sweat onto his back and I bent over and licked it off him, our two salts mixed but distinct. My own was sharp, a sea salt, but his was more mineral, full of other flavors. I licked between his shoulder blades, where his own sweat had collected, undiluted by mine.

The source of that mineral flavor, I knew, was somewhere deep inside him and I thrust farther, as far as I could reach, thinking I could find it. I pushed my right hand under him and grabbed his shaft, pulling, stroking, titillating the slit then pushing his foreskin down and caressing the base. I was deep inside him; my own prick had never seemed so long and I could feel his blood pulsing. Then he came, the sperm soaking my hand and running over and through my fingers, making a pool on the sheet. I sank into him with relief, then with a surge found I was coming myself.

We both lay there. I didn't want to pull out of him. Our

sweat glued my chest to his back. We didn't say anything. Then he turned his head so that he could see me.

"Oh, Greta, do it again," he said. I started to laugh and the movement dislodged my cock from his arse.

"Give me a couple of minutes and I will!" I said.

The amazing thing was that I did. The second time it was a battle of bodies; he wasn't passive any longer. He forced me onto my back and impaled himself on me, easing himself up and down until I grabbed him and forced him to stop. Stop, just for a moment. I wasn't ready to come again, I didn't want to come again, not until I had explored him more. We both stank and I wanted to roll in the smell.

Coming was a slower, gentler thing this time. First he came over my face as I licked his balls and he jacked himself off. Then he licked my face clean and in his saliva I caught an echo of that mineral quality I'd found in his sweat. He sat on my chest and I gazed at the small of his back as he stroked me with a careful attention. I came into his hand and he turned round and clamped his palm over my mouth, feeding me my come.

He left New York two days later, on a Sunday morning, appropriately enough. I didn't go to the airport; we would both have felt silly saying good-bye there. I stayed in bed. We kept in touch, mainly by email, but he wasn't a good correspondent. Then my attention was distracted by a painful, long passion that finally drove me to leave New York myself. Now, much calmer again, I think about what I call "the Erik time." It's like one of those perfect vacation memories, where you look back and ask yourself, "I wonder what it would be like to live there?" and you know there are far too many things about you that make it impossible. But you can't help feeling you'd like to try. He was a holiday from love and we all need a holiday sometimes.

# THE HIPPIE DOWN-LOW

Natty Soltesz

The three beautiful hippie boys passed Nate on the parkway in their chugging red Honda. He saw them only briefly but the image seared: their easy smiles, the way the late-afternoon sunlight backlit the ropes of smoke from their joint. Their lives seemed effortless and full.

And that was, in fact, the truth of it. The hippie boys had their own jokes, language, and intimate history. It formed an aura that anyone could witness but few could access.

Their Honda told the story under its mats and in the cracks of its seats. Cigarette cellophanes that once held kind buds, sticks from the ends of burnt Nag Champa, a Hacky Sack someone had lost and forgotten about. It was all there: country cruises in the back cut, late-night beer runs, outdoor summer shows.

Like Nate, the hippie boys were on their way to the Dead show at the Starlight Amphitheater, forty miles outside of Groom. But Nate was driving a year-old Grand Am, and the girl beside him, Tara, was sullen as she packed a bowl of dirt weed. It was her car. The only reason Nate was along was that she'd bought him a ticket. He was sure she had a crush on him, which only made it worse. He would've given anything to be in that golden moment with those boys, but all he could do was watch as they passed.

Tara surprised him at the show with an eighth of 'shrooms. Later, when the landscape had begun to melt and merge with the sky, Nate realized he'd lost her—ditched her, maybe. He hadn't done it on purpose, but he felt carefree for the first time that day.

Galactic was the opening band. Nate was lying on the grass wondering if the stars in the darkening sky were actually there when a boy looked down on him.

"Anything interesting up there?" he asked. He had a wide smile on his handsome, scruffy face.

"Lots," Nate said.

"I'll bet," the guy, whose name was Conrad, said. Nate started to get up, and the guy held out his hand. Nate took it. It was warm. The guy pulled him up, and Nate saw all three of them. It didn't seem possible, yet there they were.

Next to Conrad stood a pale, dreadlocked guy, named Jake, who passed a glass pipe to the third—a short but bearish guy named Bowser.

"Are they coming on soon?" Bowser said. He took a hit from the pipe and exhaled, looking at Nate through glassy eyes. "I hope they play 'Saint Stephen.' "

"They might," Jake said. Nate would've been next in line for the bowl but Jake grabbed it from Bowser's hand. "Stubby said they played it in Seattle last week." He brushed back his immaculate white-boy dreadlocks before taking a hit. " 'Saint Stephen' into 'Dark Star,' " he said through held breath.

"Oh, man, if they play 'Dark Star' I'll suck their dicks," Bowser said.

Conrad laughed. "You'll suck their dicks if they play 'Happy Birthday.' " Conrad took the bowl that Jake held out to him, but passed it to Nate instead. He smiled as Nate held the bowl to his lips. It crackled and glowed.

Conrad introduced him around. Jake shook his hand but didn't smile. Bowser seemed too fucked up to care about anything. Conrad danced next to Nate in the grass for the entire show. Once Nate considered telling him how he'd seen them earlier, how he'd envied their lives and lamented his. Then he inhaled, exhaled, and let it go.

Somehow he was still with them in the parking lot. His trip was subsiding into an electric buzz.

"Did you come with anyone?" Conrad asked. His arm kept brushing against Nate's.

"Just a girl."

"You should come party with us."

"She was my ride."

"We can be your ride," Conrad said. He was all straight teeth and floppy hair and a sinuous body that flexed under his T-shirt and shorts. "We live just outside of Groom."

"That's where I live."

"No shit?" Bowser said, stumbling beside them, a beer in one thick hand and a packed bowl in the other.

"Don't you have to go to school tomorrow?" Jake said with a sneer.

"I graduated last year," Nate said.

"Yeah, I mean, fuck it," Bowser said. He put the bowl to his lips but blew out. Pot flew everywhere.

"Aw fuck man!" Jake said. Conrad shot Nate a grin. They floated through the hiss of nitrous tanks and the murmur of the dispersing crowd. Just before they got in the Honda, Nate caught sight of Conrad cupping Bowser's butt in his hand.

An hour later they were approaching Conrad and Bowser's house, which looked to be a converted garage. There were no windows. Strange how it sat alone, and only a yard from the roadside. The front door was open and the warm light from the room wafted out onto the dark road. Any passing car could glimpse the back of a couch, an orange lamp, a wood-paneled wall covered in posters.

"You guys just leave the door open?" Nate asked as they pulled up.

"Trisha does that," Jake said.

"She's hoping some dude'll breeze in off the highway and sweep her off her feet," Bowser said.

"Fuck off," Jake said. The four of them headed inside. Trisha was lying on the couch, watching "Cops." Jake kissed her forehead.

"What the fuck took you so long?" she said, and Jake sat next to her to do damage control.

"Dude, he needs to get her the fuck out of here," Bowser said once they were in the kitchen. He grabbed three beers from the fridge.

"Stacy's coming to pick her up after work, just relax," Conrad said. Nate took a drink from the beer. It was ice cold and hoppy. "So Nate, who was the girl who took you to the show?" Conrad asked.

"Nobody. Just a friend."

"And you left her there?" Bowser said. He held out his beer and Nate clinked it with his. "That's awesome."

From the living room came Trisha's cigarette-roughened voice. "I fucking *told* you I don't care," she said. Jake was muttering: "Baby, baby…"

"Do whatever the fuck you want," she continued. "You will anyway."

"Love…" Conrad said.

Once Trisha was gone Jake lightened up considerably, packing copious bowls of some of the best weed Nate had ever smoked. Jake found Nate to be a willing audience for his opinions on weed—the best strains and the effects of various growing conditions and other facts that were meant to impress. Nate was just happy to be on his good side.

There was an undercurrent in the room that Nate couldn't place. It could have been from the mushrooms, but it felt more anxious than that. It felt sexual; not that he was schooled in such matters—Nate was a virgin. Basically.

Junior year he'd let his girlfriend at the time, Sara, blow him at a keg party on Derry Lane. He'd managed to cum by thinking about Woody Harrelson. Sara went off to college in Arizona a month later and he was relieved to have dodged any further bullets.

Now Nate was working at NovaStar, a telephone survey gig in Latrobe, and living with his parents in Groom. He had work friends, including Tara, and they'd spend evenings driving around and getting high. Something was missing. They were his friends by default, since everyone else had split. He'd remained, in a netherworld between high school and whatever came next.

"*No more beer*," Bowser said, cutting off Jake's soliloquy on the mechanics of a superior gravity bong. "What are we gonna do now?" He was gnawing on a cube of raw ramen.

"Truth or dare?" Conrad said.

"Who goes first?" Bowser said.

"You do 'cause you asked," Jake said.

"Fuck that—the new guy! You have to pick one—truth or dare?" Bowser slurred.

"Truth, I guess."

"You pussy!"

"Shut up, Bowser," Conrad said. "Okay, truth...how many times a day do you jerk off?"

"I don't know. Maybe once?"

"You're shittin' me," Bowser said.

"I live with my parents..."

"That's no excuse."

"Jake next," Conrad said. "Truth or dare?"

"Truth."

Bowser cut in: "Have you ever fucked Trisha in the ass?"

"You think she'd let me near that?"

"Huge surprise," Conrad said.

"Me next!" Bowser said. "Dare dare dare."

"Okay..." Conrad said, with a glance at Nate. "I dare you to make out with Jake." Bowser shrugged. Jake leaned in. Bowser pulled Jake's head to his and mashed their mouths together. It wasn't silly—there was tongue on both sides. It was a jolt to Nate's whole body. Everything changed.

They broke apart. Bowser wiped his mouth. Jake pulled back his dreads and secured them with an elastic band. He looked at Nate and laughed.

"I think we blew his mind. Conrad's next."

"Dare," Conrad said.

"Make out with Nate," Bowser said. Nate had known it was coming. Conrad looked at him.

"Shall we?" he said, stepping toward him. Nate leaned forward. It was easy, Nate thought. How could it have been so easy this whole time? Their lips met, then their tongues, and there was nothing and everything to it. Conrad's mouth tasted sharp like cigarettes. Their bodies came together. Conrad wrapped his arms around Nate's back, bringing them closer still, and all of it went straight to Nate's dick.

Then it was over. Bowser and Jake were clapping and whistling.

"Look, he's totally hard," Jake said, pointing at the front of Nate's shorts.

"Take it out, man," Bowser said.

"Leave him alone," Conrad said.

"Fuck that, I'll show mine," Bowser said. He yanked down the front of his patched pants, showing his dense auburn pubes and a fat, perky cock that bounced in the air.

"Yeah, but that's not what we wanna see," Jake said, and spun him around. Bowser braced himself against the counter as Jake pulled Bowser's pants down over his ass. It was a big, firm beauty. "Spread it, dude—show the new guy." Bowser kicked off his pants and spread his legs. Jake gave the ass a slap. "That's the stuff right there," he said, fondling himself through his gauze pants.

Nate watched in a daze. Of course it had all been leading up to this. Conrad had taken off his shorts and was now stroking a respectably thick cock that hung from a thatch of jet black pubes. Jake was untying his pants.

"Here comes the big reveal," Conrad said. Bowser turned around eagerly. Jake let his pants fall to the floor—he wasn't wearing underwear. Hanging there was the biggest dick Nate could've imagined. It looked like a submarine. The thickness of it tapered at the head, which was uncut and half-sheathed, the head slick and moist. "Something, isn't it?"

"Don't be afraid," Bowser said. He took Nate's hand and brought it to Jake's dick. Nate wrapped his fingers around the thing, which was hot, pulsing, and alive. "Biggest dick in the

Conemaugh Valley," Bowser said. Nobody laughed. Nate hefted it in his palm, let it glide back and forth. Jake was smiling at him. He seemed used to the attention.

"You can try sucking it," Conrad said. Nate looked up. "If you want." Nate paused. It was too much, with the three of them looking at him like that.

"Don't mind if I do," Bowser said, taking Jake's cock from him. He dropped to his knees and pointed the cock at his open maw. Holding Jake's balls with his other hand he gobbled down the dick, all the way to the base. Jake's lungs deflated. Bowser went for another pass, then another, his tongue curling underneath.

Nate became aware of Conrad moving next to him.

"You *are* hard," he said in his ear, reaching down to feel. "Mind if I take it out?" Nate didn't answer, and Conrad slipped his hand underneath Nate's shorts and around his dick. "Feel mine," he said. Nate reached back and took it in his hand. He turned around and their mouths connected. Conrad dropped Nate's shorts to the floor. They held on to each other's arms and pressed their naked cocks together. Nate could hear Bowser slurping on Jake's cock, Jake's increasingly labored breathing.

When he looked up he saw that Bowser was bent over the counter again. Jake knelt before him, his head buried between the big melon cheeks of Bowser's butt. Bowser groaned low and long.

Jake stood and drummed his meat against Bowser's ass.

"Who's gonna do the honors?" Jake said.

"He doesn't care," Conrad said, reaching over to caress Bowser's asscheek. "Slut'll take anything that comes his way." He gave the cheek a slap. Bowser remained prone, his ass presented to them.

"What about this?" Jake said, picking up a beer bottle. He

swigged the dregs then got the mouth and neck of the bottle slobbery. He spread one of Bowser's cheeks and brought the bottle to his asshole. "Watch," he said to Nate, and pressed it in. Bowser groaned as the bottle entered him. Jake pushed it as far as it could go. He took his hand away and the bottle stayed. Jake and Conrad chuckled.

"You wanna try it?" Jake said, looking to Nate. Nate kicked off his shorts and went over to Bowser, taking the base of the bottle in his hand. He could feel the tight grip of Bowser's asshole around the bottle's neck as he pulled it out then in. "No need to be gentle," Jake said, taking the bottle from Nate. He jammed it hard and steady, and Bowser only whimpered and backed up for more.

Conrad left and came back with a huge pump-top bottle of lube. He set it on the counter. Jake reached over and squirted some in his palm.

"What are you doing?" Conrad said.

"First dibs, man—you got it last time."

"New guy gets first dibs," Conrad said.

"Whatever," Jake said, grimacing. "Here, let me see your dick." He took hold of Nate's cock with his lubed palm and got it slick. Then he removed the bottle from Bowser's ass and set it on the counter with a clink. He put more lube on Bowser's hole. "He's ready for you, dude. Have at it."

"Relax, man. I don't think he's done this before," Conrad said.

"No way," Jake said. Nate blushed.

"Don't worry about it, buddy," Conrad whispered in Nate's ear. "Go as slow or fast as you want—don't sweat it if you pop quick."

"Fuck him, man," Jake said.

"*Somebody* fuck me," Bowser said. Conrad helped get Nate's

dick inside. The heat was what struck him—like a rolled-up electric blanket. It was tight, too. He felt like he should hold still and get his bearings, but some instinct took over and he backed out, then shoved it right back in. He was drunk, high and tripping, and Bowser's ass was drawing him in like water down a drain.

Jake had reached underneath Bowser and was whacking him off. "He's gonna shoot already," he said of Nate.

Conrad said in Nate's ear: "Cum inside him, man—lube it up for the next guy."

"I think he's already cumming," Jake said, and it was true. Nate's juice had just spilled out of him, the tenor of the room so pitched that it felt like the continuation of a sustained climax.

He was done so he slid out. Conrad clapped him on the shoulder. Jake had taken his place and was making a show of slapping his boner against Bowser's sloppy hole.

"Behold the master at work," Conrad said. "At least he'd like to think so." There was no denying that Bowser perked up when he felt Jake's hog at his back door, a fact that made Nate feel slightly inadequate. Bowser spread his cheeks and waited. Finally Jake slid it home.

"*Fuck*," Bowser cried out. Jake's fuck was showy; he ran his hands through his dreads, flexed his abs as he swung his hips in slick little thrusts. Nate watched, amazed at the sight of something so large breaching something so small, the rim of Bowser's asshole stretching elastically around Jake's cock.

Jake went on for a good ten minutes before he stepped aside to give Conrad a turn.

"Wish me luck," Conrad said to Nate. Hot as it had been to watch Jake's big dick pierce Bowser's butt, Nate liked watching Conrad the best. Conrad really seemed to enjoy himself, varying his thrusts between quick jabs with the head and long pistons inward. He clutched Bowser's torso as he screwed, sliding his dick all the way out, poising it at the entrance, and driving it back inside. Jake did the duty of jerking Bowser off, the three of them going at it like a well-oiled machine, or maybe just a well-practiced routine.

Conrad was obviously going for the gold. His thrusts got faster and his face flushed red.

"Oh, man, he's blowing," Jake said of Bowser. Conrad took hold of Bowser's ass and pounded it even more savagely. His eyes found Nate's. He was breathing like a locomotive and it was obvious he was cumming. "Yeah, man, cream that ass," Jake was saying, but Conrad's eyes never left Nate's, not even after he'd finished, relaxing his body onto Bowser's, catching his breath. He gave Bowser's butt a slap and slid out.

"Thanks for the good time," he said.

"Whenever, chief," Bowser said, turning around. His cock dripped on the linoleum as he walked to the fridge. He chugged a carton of orange juice.

"Guess you're spending the night," Conrad said to Nate.

They said goodnight to the others. Bowser shook his hand and said, "Good job."

"You'll get better," Jake said. Still half-hard, he led Bowser to the couch. Apparently the party wasn't over yet.

Conrad motioned for Nate to follow him. Just before they turned down the hall, Nate looked back to realize the front door was still open.

From the road you could see inside: just enough to make you wonder.

# THE STRAY

David May

*Some are more human than others.*
—Stevie Smith

Bud was discovered, as strays often are, wet, cold, and shivering in the back patio of the Seattle Eagle. It was commonly assumed that Bud had had parents and a family at some time in his life, and even a proper name, but none of this information was forthcoming. Stories spread rapidly that he'd been kidnapped and imprisoned and had only just managed to escape with his life, but with no memory of life prior to his enslavement (for cable television had supplied numerous such stories to draw on); or that he was the victim of some cruel Master who, having provided Bud with a brain injury, abandoned his amnesiac slave to Fate. While none of the scenarios being woven about his past proved to be true, neither was there ever a satisfactory explanation of Bud's beginnings.

The facts were these: the day manager found Bud huddled in

the back of the bar's patio. Being a kind man, the day manager knelt beside him and asked, "What's your name, bud?"

And from that moment, he answered to Bud.

The bar's manager and staff then took it upon themselves to look after Bud, to feed and clothe him, to keep him warm and safe—just until he was able to tell them what had happened. Bud, it should be noted, had an almost unearthly handsomeness, with a compact, well-muscled, furry body; high cheekbones, and devastating green eyes complemented by a sexy scruffiness that appeared permanent. Being that sexy and that handsome, as well as agreeable, his presence was something of a commodity. Soon Bud was working at the door of the Eagle on weekends and sometimes as a towel boy at the bathhouse across the street. Customers were charmed by his guileless pleasure in being admired, to say nothing of his willingness to provide whatever pleasure his admirers might ask of him. Thus he was treated kindly, as strays often are when they are both beautiful and agreeable.

In no time, he was collared and well cared for by a Sir who saw in Bud all that was wild and wonderful in the world. He treated Bud gently but firmly, and Bud thrived under his care. Already free with his body, Bud had no qualms about repaying the Sir's kindness with whatever sexual reciprocation was required of him. Sir loved Bud deeply, and when he learned that he had pancreatic cancer, he took steps to be certain that someone would take care of Bud after his death.

When Sir died, Bud didn't weep, but uttered primal cries of despair. He wandered about the apartment looking for someone he knew would never return, burying his face in Sir's pillow and finding comfort in what remained of the man's scent. He was adopted then, as strays frequently are when orphaned, by Sir's friends, a couple known as the Bills. Bud slept between them, or in a pile of blankets on the floor, accepting their attentions, sexual and otherwise, with a kind of acquiescence that they found touching. In addition to cleaning house for the Bills (and Bud was nothing if not obsessed with cleanliness) and working in their garden, Bud continued to work at the Eagle on weekend nights, as a bathhouse towel boy on other nights, and as a purveyor of pleasure when the occasion arrived. Downstairs in the Bills' playroom, Bud built himself a nook to sleep in. Closeted there, snug and secure in the dark he felt at home in, he slept through most of Seattle's wet winter days. When the weather was fine, he slept naked, stretched out across a blanket on the back lawn, abandoning himself to the sun as if it were his only lover.

Late at night Bud would wander Capitol Hill, deftly leaping into trees, padding gently across rooftops, or gracefully running along back fences. When the moon was full, he would sit on the rooftop and stare at it for hours, finding comfort in the cold light and the smells of the night. Then he'd stretch, and gracefully, almost silently, leap to a tree, then the fence, and finally the wet, dewy earth. Shaking the pads of his feet dry, Bud quietly returned to the warmth of the Bills' bed, where he would sleep succored by the scent and warmth of the men who had taken over his care.

When awake, Bud watched the world around him with constant curiosity, alert to subtle shifts in his surroundings. He listened carefully to every word said within his earshot, sometimes repeating what had been said word for word weeks, or even months, later. Other than these few odd habits (odd habits not being uncommon among strays), Bud smiled when expected to smile and laughed when it was proper to laugh. In short, he seemed not quite normal, but normal enough, and content with his life.

Years passed, and one May the Bills decided to take Bud with them to Chicago for International Mr. Leather. They had gone in previous years, off and on, but had been disinclined to spend their money on Bud's airfare and food, leaving Bud at home to take care of himself. When they returned, Bud was happy to see them, seeking some sign of affection—a slap on the ass, a cock down his throat, a fierce dry fuck while he bent over the toilet—to assure himself that he was still loved. This year, however, the Bills realized that they were losing their edge, having passed the peak of their appeal as Daddies, and decided to bring Bud with them, thus securing for themselves the status of Slave Owners, and so increasing their desirability.

Bud did not take easily to being on a leash, but complied despite his desire to run free. Being led about, dressed in new gear (rubber, leather, camouflage), on display, was not something he was well suited to, but neither was being punished, so he obeyed. Not liking the crowds at the event, Bud would, when surrounded by so many admiring strangers, lean into one or both of the Bills for safety. For this he was teased but fondly caressed, and so it became a part of his strategy for survival in the noisy vastness of the hotel's lobby. That the Bills sometimes sold his ass to strangers was of less concern to him than that he not be restrained or caged, so he remained docile while keeping an eye on the exit, a ploy common to strays whose survival depends on the kindness of others.

Late Saturday night, after an orgy that might have exhausted others (an orgy to which the Bills' entrance had only been made possible by their ownership of so beautiful a boy), Bud's owners collapsed into bed, snoring away almost as soon as their heads hit their pillows. Bud, accidentally left unfettered for the night, removed the leash and most of his clothes before exploring the halls and stairwells of the enormous hotel. He sniffed the air hoping to find what he was looking for, what he sensed was waiting for him.

He found men in every out-of-the-way corner, singly or in groups, wherever he looked, men unused to so much stimulus and unable to sleep for fear they miss something, men stumbling back to their beds after a night of dreamlike debauchery, men waiting in the doors of their rooms hoping for one more fuck. Some of these men reached out to him, called to him with thick, urgent voices, but Bud ignored them. They were not what he sought; they were not the one he knew was so near.

He entered the lobby bar with reluctance, even as his instincts urged him forward. A good number of men still congregated there during the late hour, some of them sad enough to earn Bud's sympathy. He moved lithely through the milling men, eyes and ears alert. Some were laughing too loudly, some sobbing into oversized cocktails over a lover's faithlessness; others basked in the glow of so many men, absorbing the pheromones that filled the air. And there, in the center of it all, was the one Bud sought, the one he'd sensed was there since his arrival two days before.

Bud stood and stared. The man stared back.

The man was tall, powerfully built, thick legged, and almost impossibly muscular. His sandy blond mane of thick hair was in need of cutting; a full beard covered his face almost up to the cheekbones. His mouth was large and sensual; his brown eyes glinted yellow when the light caught them; his bare arms, chest, and back were thickly matted with fur.

Someone said something funny, and he laughed, his laugh a roar, his chuckle a very loud purr. Surrounded by admirers, the man accepted their homage with a graceful acquiescence, gently touching one or another of them in their conversation, slapping another manfully on the back. Through all this camaraderie, though, he remained aloof, waiting as he was for Bud to find him. Very calmly leaving his flock of admirers, the stranger approached Bud, gently touching the small of Bud's back, stepping close to Bud before whispering, "There's my little bro."

Bud's heart stopped in his throat.

"Are you my brother?"

"You didn't know?"

"Big bro?"

"That's right."

There was a kiss, gentle and deep, strong and tender, that laid claim to Bud as neither Sir nor the Bills had ever done. Big Bro put a hand on Bud's tightly covered ass and walked away with him amidst the applause, the *ohs* and *ahs* and laughter of those who had hoped for Big Bro's attention and now wished that they could watch the coupling to come.

Big Bro led Bud out of the hotel and hailed a cab. Nearly naked, Bud wrapped himself around Big Bro more for protection than for warmth in the night's quite cool spring air, hiding what was exposed from an uncertain world. The cab raced along the lake, Bud nestling into the vast furriness of Big Bro's chest, Big Bro stroking Bud's scruffy cheeks and chuckling so loudly that it sounded more than ever like a purr.

When they reached their destination, a tower overlooking the lake, its height threatening to scrape the sky with fairy tale–like accuracy, Big Bro led Bud by the hand inside and up the elevator to a vista frequented more by birds than men.

Bud stared into the open space beyond the window for several minutes, watching the moon's reflection on the lake that was so much like a small sea. Big Bro wrapped his arms around Bud, nibbling Bud's ear, caressing Bud's nipples, purring.

"Is this my new home, Big Brother?"

"Yes, little bro. This is where you belong."

Bud knelt and removed his boots and socks, then the tight leather shorts that had been his only other clothing. Kneeling before Big Bro, he undid the button fly and pulled aside the leather jeans to better see what was to possess him. Unleashed suddenly from the confines of the leather, the thick phallus slapped Bud sharply across the face. Bud flinched slightly before opening his mouth and inhaling Big Bro's mammoth member to the root. Big Bro rocked back and forth on his booted feet, his gloved hands caressing the back of Bud's head as he pushed his cock in and out of Bud's throat.

"Oh, little bro, oh, little bro..."

The rhythm of the rocking increased in speed, and Big Bro's murmurs became more guttural. Holding the back of Bud's head, he fucked Bud's mouth long and hard until, screaming, he exploded and shot his seed down Bud's anxious and hungry throat. Bud felt the head of the cock expand and burst, felt the ribbons of manhood cascade down his throat, and he eagerly swallowed even as the still hard cock was removed from his mouth.

After Big Bro had come to himself and had caught his breath, he knelt down next to Bud and kissed him with more longing than he had before, with more desire, more love. He held Bud close, letting their furry pelts rub against each other, kissing Bud, licking the sweat from Bud's face and neck. Bud responded in kind, purring with pleasure at the rough texture of his lover's tongue as it scraped against his skin and fur. He helped Big Bro out of his boots, leather jeans, harness, armbands and gloves. Licking the hairy flesh as it was newly exposed, making Big Bro purr in return, Bud sought only to please him, to mark him as his own, even as Big Bro had marked him.

Big Bro dove into Bud's hairy ass, parting the furry cheeks with his huge paws while his tongue sought the musk of Bud's sex, the new center of his own joy. On his stomach, Bud felt the rough tongue pluming the depths of his fuck hole, and kneaded the carpet just as Big Bro's paws were kneading his buttcheeks. Bud lost himself in the pleasure of the grooming, of the bearded face against his furry buttcheeks, in the need mounting in his own loins.

Bud was roughly turned over onto his back, his legs wrapping themselves over Big Bro's broad, hirsute shoulders. Big Bro's cock found its target and entered the snug cavern where so many men had spilled their spawn, but which would now make room only for Big Bro's essence. He entered slowly, ever alert for whatever sensations were revealed in his lover's face, as eager to please as to be pleased. Bud gasped, only partly from the pain of being split so roughly apart, and partly from anticipation of the coming ecstasy. He nodded, and Big Bro pushed forward, slowly sliding into the hairy hole, into the depths of Bud's body and soul.

The scent of their pheromones thickened the air around them, adding to the urgency of their need to couple, to climax face-to-face, to know and share the agony of the coming climax. They kissed roughly as they fucked, their teeth clashing together while their tongues wrestled for control. Big Bro pushed forward as Bud met each thrust with his own, his cock arching high into the air as Big Bro's manhood drove deeper and faster into Bud's body.

They came together. Big Bro's cock once again exploded, expanding and stretching the confines of Bud's guts. With Big Bro's final thrust, Bud's body arched toward the ceiling as he ejaculated, covering them both with cum. What Big Bro couldn't catch in his mouth, he licked from the matted hair on Bud's body, even as Bud returned the favor by cleaning Big Bro's sweaty body.

They slept that night curled together on the floor, their bodies intertwined for the comfort of each other's company as much as for warmth in the now chilly room. When they awoke, Bud prepared their breakfast, after which they spent an hour grooming each other before a short nap. When Big Bro stretched his body, he found Bud at the window keenly watching high-flying birds race past the apartment. He nuzzled Bud from behind, his cock poking at its new home.

"How old are you, Big Bro?"

"Don't know. Why? Do you know how old you are?"

"No. I never bothered to count."

"Not to worry, little bro, Big Bro will look after you now. Big Bro will protect you and keep you safe, and Big Bro will never put you on a leash."

Bud leaned his torso forward and pushed his butt back to find and engulf Big Bro's cock. That was all he needed to know.

When the Bills woke up the next morning and found Bud had vanished, they wondered where he had gone, but didn't worry at first. As the hours passed, they became frantic, showing his picture to everyone and anyone. Finally, on the morning of their departure, someone recognized Bud from the fuzzy image on the mobile phone.

"Yeah, a couple nights ago he went off with this guy, big ol' lion of a guy."

"Where did they go?"

The man shrugged his shoulders and nodded to the front door of the hotel.

On the flight home, the Bills comforted themselves with the thought that strays sometimes disappear.

# I WISH

Richard Hennebert

It is nine P.M. on a Saturday, and you are in the mood to go out, but your boyfriend is too tired. You insist. He refuses. Instead he suggests a Daniel Craig DVD and a tub of Strawberry Häagen-Dazs. You don't even bother.

You go to the kitchen and grab a can of beer from the fridge. Alcohol is what you want and what you need. And a fag, but you gave them up since the ban. You plan to buy a pack of Marlboro Lights on your way to the bus stop; you have just made the decision to go out. You pick up the phone and dial your best friend. He is already with some mates in a Vauxhall bar. You can be there in less than thirty minutes.

You can smell your armpits. Your smell is sexy so you don't wash. You drink another beer to calm your nerves after a tiff with the boyfriend. You head for the bathroom where you strip naked. You put on a cock ring, brush your teeth, and splash cold water on your face. No aftershave. You walk to the bedroom and open the sex drawer, where you find your rubber shorts. You put a pair of jeans over them and pull on a T-shirt. It is fairly mild for mid-September so you don't need a jacket. You slip your keys, some cash and a bottle of poppers in your pockets and slam the front door to end the argument. You finish the can of beer and toss it in a bin before reaching the newsagent. On the way to the bus stop you light up a cigarette. You feel alive again, alive because you are about to do something bad. You feel drunk on ill-gotten freedom.

On the 185 bus to Vauxhall you watch lonely people waiting for a different bus, clutching Tesco bags. You see the inside of lit living rooms with families watching reality on TV. You hear sirens and people shouting. You notice a few lads with short hair like you, heading to the clubs, like you.

Your mates in the bar are pissed. You need to catch up and order a beer with a shot. The barman with only a pair of trunks on is hot: nipples pierced, a tattoo above his crotch. He notices you adjusting your erection. Your mates are on their way to another bar. You drink your beer in the street and have another cigarette. Your mates haven't bothered hiding their outfits: leather chaps, chains, cop caps, harnesses. They sniff poppers and smoke cigars.

In the next bar, you head for the loo. The ladies' is empty but you prefer queuing for the gents'. The music fades when the door is shut. Some men check their hair, others linger. You head for a urinal. You manage to piss despite your semierection, eyeing both sides for what's on offer. The man on your right has a full erection. You step back and leave. Your fourth beer and a shot numb your inhibition.

It is past eleven-thirty, time for the Pig.

There is a queue. Your mates crack jokes. You laugh. Other strangers laugh, too. You suddenly remember that you belonged to this community. You have missed it. Your recent life in your cozy home with your doctor boyfriend isn't for you. You offer cigarettes all around. You smoke your last one before you go in.

You split from your mates and find a locker in a quiet corner. You take off your jeans and T-shirt. You keep the key in your boots, with some cash. You put the bottle of poppers inside your rubber shorts.

Your mates have bought you a beer. You explore the place under the arches with them. The last tube rumbles underfoot.

There's barely any light. You see giant screens with sado-masochistic porn. Your mates carry on. You stay. This is when the other side of you truly comes to life. There is a grin on your face while watching the film. Yeah. You are no longer a punter having a beer in a seedy London club. You are the fucker on the screen. It is you out there on the giant porn screen. You are the porn star. Your darkest fantasies have been unleashed.

You finish your beer in sloppy gulps, drop the empty can and head for the stairs.

You feel the sweaty bodies against your skin. You feel extremely horny, but you resist. It is part of the fun. Your insides burn with such vivacity that it is almost painful. Your blood is pumping so violently that you can hear it in your head, but you resist. You kiss lips and bite nipples. You touch erect dicks in the semidarkness. You join orgies. You slap chests, bums, backs. Yet you resist. You push away those hands that try and enter your rubber pants, those fingers that stroke your dick. You resist because you are in control. You float on the surface of pure pleasure, that ocean of sensations and anticipation. You help men come. Their spunk trickles down your bare legs. They groan in your ear. They beg on their knees but you still resist.

You leave the space and go downstairs, to the basement. There is a maze in front of you. You assume there are areas with slings, baths, glory holes, and other instruments of torture/pleasure. You are right. There is no music, only the symphony of moans mingled with whispers.

You head for the maze. Your body exudes virility as your muscles are pumped up, your skin shines with sweat and semen and your erection is peaking the black rubber of your shorts. A guy asks you for some poppers. You sniff and share and then walk into the sexual inferno.

You touch and smell but push bodies away because you can't find the fantasy trapped in your head. Let it fly out for you to see it better. From a distance you see it.

From a distance you see him.

He is not alone. He is surrounded by older men who piss on him. One has his dick shoved inside his mouth. The young lad is choking on it. You find that exciting. A fist is being inserted inside him. His face is contorted. You move closer. The older men move away. The young lad, give him eighteen, is choking on his leash. You pull your shorts down and grab him from behind, holding him by his leather collar. You tighten your grip. You thrust. The smell of poppers is intoxicating. You hold life in your hands; living flesh between your fingers.

His hands reach for a buckle he can't unfasten. He inserts his fingers behind it. He has no desire to take it off. His head rolls; the dizziness is part of the game. You know at this point that climax could be murderous but you don't care. You could ruin your entire life for a few seconds of pure ecstasy and yet you do not let go. It feels so good, so good that you come inside the young lad. He turns around and cleans the spunk off your hard dick with his tongue.

You are alive.

# THE SUBURBAN BOY

Simon Sheppard

They were stopped at a traffic light, in front of a church with a sign out front urging ACCEPT JESUS!

"The exclamation point is a bit pushy, don't you think?" Nathan said.

"Well, Christianity didn't get where it is today by being Christian," Rich replied. Central Florida, beyond the gates of the Magic Kingdom, was turning out to be rather old school, God-guts-and-gunwise, which was either refreshing or distressing, depending.

"Did you see that?" Rich asked, a couple of blocks later.

"The boy with the buckteeth?"

"Well, the rest of him was nice. Especially the legs."

"The land that orthodontia forgot."

"He looked like a hustler."

"Here? In the middle of the middle of Florida? Don't be silly." Nathan swung the steering wheel to the right.

"Well, he was just standing there by the side of the road."

"This isn't Santa Monica Boulevard."

"Obviously." The single word fairly dripped with sarcasm; the visit to Nathan's mother and brother had been pretty much a disaster, and nerves were frayed.

After a silence, Nathan asked, "Do you want to go back?"

"I don't think so."

"Back for him?"

"I don't think so."

But once they got to the motel they'd moved into when bunking at Nathan's boyhood home had gotten too dispiriting, Rich said, "Yes, let's do it. Let's go back."

"He'll be gone."

"Let's see," Rich replied. "It's just a few minutes away."

They walked out of their only moderately depressing room, got in the rented Kia, and drove back the way that they'd come.

The boy was still there, standing pointlessly on the sidewalk, at an intersection a couple of blocks from the 441. Rich was right: The young man did have excellent legs.

"Let's see what, if anything, happens," Rich said. Nathan turned the corner, pulled onto the shoulder, and sat there idling. The boy noticed them, but still stood there, shifting slightly from foot to foot. Finally Rich thought, *This is stupid*, and raised his hand in ambiguous greeting. The boy smiled slightly, his teeth even more prominent, then walked over to the car.

"How y'all doing?" he said. His voice was surprisingly high and melodious; if he had been working Santa Monica, the Southern drawl would most likely have been an affectation.

"Good. Want to go for a ride?" Even to himself, Rich sounded pathetically clichéd. But the boy reached for the handle of the back door; he was either aimlessly bored, or, indeed, on the game.

Rich glanced over his shoulder; there was some semivaluable stuff on the backseat. "Let me get back there with you," he said. If the boy thought that was the least bit unusual, he didn't show it.

Once Nathan pulled out, Rich stared at the stranger sitting next to him. Maybe the first thing Nathan had noticed about him was his misaligned teeth, but the rest of his face was perfectly lovely, in an attractive-but-ordinary way. And his legs *were* nice—big calves, thighs muscular but not too bulky, all covered with a pelt of dark blond hair. Rich took a deep breath: a blend of sunshine and sweat. "So..." he began, then didn't know what to say next. They were back at the ACCEPT JESUS! church.

"So what are y'all's names?" the boy finally drawled. "I'm Bobby."

"I'm Jonathan," Rich said, "and my friend there is David." He figured that Bobby wasn't the kid's real name, either.

"Pleased to meet ya." The boy leaned back, put his hands behind his head, sighed, and spread his legs. His shiny basketball shorts were bulging at the crotch; in any case, Bobby (or whoever) was pretty clearly no dewy-eyed innocent.

"So how old are you?" Nathan asked from the front seat. He was afraid of the answer, but hell, nothing had happened yet, and he could always pull over and let the boy out.

"Nineteen."

"Nineteen?" Nathan sounded, Rich thought, a bit too skeptical for his own good. But the boy was already pulling his wallet out of his back pocket, showing his ID to Rich. He was, in fact, four months past nineteen, and his name really was Bobby. Rich was sorry the boy had shifted from his seductive former position, but he was glad he wasn't jailbait.

"So were you standing in front of your house?" Rich asked.

"Nah. I just go over to that corner to...hang out. Y'know?"

Nathan and Rich thought they did.

They'd just driven past a Publix when Bobby, surprisingly, reached over and grabbed Rich's jeans-clad knee. "So what do you fellas want to do?"

"Oh, I don't know," Rich said, aiming for a tone somewhere between "nonchalant" and "client." The boy's hand moved up his leg. "Go back to our motel and get to know each other?" Rich had gotten a hard-on; he couldn't help himself.

Bobby's touch moved a few more inches crotchward. "You guys generous?"

"You a cop?" Nathan asked.

That seemed to amuse Bobby no end. "Oh, Jesus fuck, no," he laughed. "I'm not. Two hundred?"

"One?"

Bobby took his hand off Rich's leg, leaned back again, and started kneading his own impressive crotch. "One-fifty."

"One twenty-five," Nathan haggled.

"One-fifty. Firm." Bobby moved his hand away from his crotch. Rich could see it was firm indeed.

"Okay, one-fifty," Rich said. Why quibble?

Bobby smiled. "So let's go have some fun."

And there it was. Settled.

Daddy was drunk again. When Mama came home from working her half shift at Wal-Mart, there he was, passed out on a kitchen chair, kind of propped up. Right in the middle of the afternoon. At least he hadn't pissed himself.

She poked him, hard, he came to, and then the screaming started. I hid out in my room for a while, then decided it was time to go make some cash. If they ever knew, they'd kill me, but fuck it. I want to get out. I need to get out. And in this economy, what kind of a shit-ass job could a high-school dropout like me get? Nothing. Nothing. Fuck-all.

I'd felt like jacking off when I got up, but I'd never gotten around to it, so I was pretty damn horny. I changed into a pair of b-ball shorts, no underwear, and a fairly new wifebeater, and headed out. Mama saw me leaving.

"Where you going, Bobby?" she asked, sounding like she really couldn't care less.

"Just out," I called back from the doorway. "Be back pretty soon."

And I walked down to where I usually do, liking the feeling of my dick slapping against my thigh as I walked. Only I started getting hard, so I had to stop for a minute until it went down.

The day was still hot, and I started to sweat. When I got to the street I just stood there, not doing nothing noticeable, in case the cops passed by. After all, it still ain't illegal to just stand by the side of the road.

There were a few false alarms—guys who slowed down or stopped for a second and then drove off, like their conscience was getting the better of them. Like they had been driving home to their wives.

But then this black Korean car pulls up and stops right around the corner. I thought maybe I'd seen it before, going the other way, and now it's back. There are two guys in it; the passenger, the one toward me, rolls down his window and kind of looks me over. Bingo.

After a second I walk over. "Hey," I say, "you guys looking for some fun?"

The one on my side damn near is drooling all over himself. "Fuck yeah," he says. "Fuck yeah." They're pretty damn old, but they're not bad looking, neither of them.

"Then stop farting around and let me in your damn car."

Well, that does it. The driver—he's a redhead, the other one has black hair—unlocks the doors. But as I'm getting in, the dark-haired one gets out of his door and jumps into the backseat, which has some shit sitting on it that he shoves aside.

"How much?" the guy who's now beside me asks. He already has his hand up my shorts.

"Hundred fifty."

The guy nods and says, "Okay." Makes me think I should have asked for more.

"Hey," I say, since the guy already has his hand on my dick and is kneading away, "let's go somewhere, okay?"

"You a cop?" the driver says.

I laugh. "Fuck no." If he only knew how far from a cop I am. But I guess he thought he had to ask. By this time—I'll admit it—my cock's nice and hard. "Let's go," I say again.

"You sure you want to?" the driver asks. He's asking his friend, not me.

"I'm sure," the guy next to me says. He sure knows how to jack a dude off.

The driver doesn't say nothing else, just pulls away from the curb.

The motel was one of those old-fashioned jobbies where all the rooms could be accessed by outside stairs and walkways, so, fortunately, Rich and Nathan didn't have to smuggle their charge past the basilisk gaze of the day clerk, an unfriendly old woman with dyed-orange hair and a rhinestone American flag pin on her plus-sized floral-print dress.

Rich led the way into the room, followed by Bobby. Nathan brought up the rear; after the three of them were inside, he locked the door. The lock made a clunk. The room hadn't been cleaned yet and they hadn't made the bed that morning, though the second bed stood untouched. *Now he's going to know that we sleep together,* Nathan thought. Like it mattered.

Like it mattered at all.

The boy looked from one man to the other for a few seconds, then flopped on the bed, his crotch thrust upward. Rich walked over and stood between his legs.

"Money first," Bobby said.

Rich reached down and touched the boy's furry leg, right above the knee.

"I mean it. Show me the money first." The toothy smile vanished from Bobby's face.

Rich backed off and reached for his wallet. He'd just gone to the ATM that morning, but he still didn't have enough. "You got fifty bucks, David?" He wasn't sure, come to think of it, whether Nathan was supposed to be "David" or "Jonathan." Whatever; the boy sure as hell hadn't kept track either.

"Forty."

"Hey..." Bobby sounded like he was suddenly angry.

"Listen," Nathan said, hoping things wouldn't get ugly. There were two of them, one of the boy, but still...he'd heard stories. Why had Rich insisted on... "If you want, I'll go out, find an ATM. But it's just ten bucks."

Bobby paused—Nathan thought he could actually see him thinking.

"Aw, hell," he said at last. "Let's do it." His cock was visibly hard beneath the shiny fabric of his shorts. Rich relaxed and reached down again. Bobby spread his legs wider. Rich looked up at Nathan, who was standing a few feet away, an indecipherable look on his face.

"You want some of this?" Rich asked.

"You go ahead. I'll watch for now."

Rich always does this. Well, not *always*. But a lot. Too fucking much.

Gets us into messes that I'm not ready for. Was the kid kind of cute, standing there on the side of the road? Well, yeah. So what? That didn't mean that he was a hustler. And even when that's exactly what he turned out to be, that doesn't mean we had to invite him back to our motel.

And then when we get here, the kid already sprawled backward on our bed, the front of his stupid basketball shorts tented out, it turns out that Rich doesn't even have enough money to pay for him. *Damn it,* I want to say, *clean up your own messes.* But I pay the extra forty dollars. It was supposed to be fifty, actually, and when the little whore finds out he's not going to get everything he'd asked for, this threatening look passes across his face, like it isn't above him to kill us for ten bucks. And that's the first time I start getting hard all day.

After the money shit gets straightened out, Rich swoops down. That seems kind of stupid, since I've always figured the hustler was supposed to service the client, not the other way around. But, hey, my experience in that area isn't what you'd call extensive. Rich starts stroking the kid's legs, then moves up to his basket. The boy's dick is obviously a big one. Rich clambers up on the bed and buries his face in the kid's crotch. I can see that he's wrapping his lips around the still-hidden hard-on. The boy pulls up his wifebeater and starts to stroke his own chest, which is surprisingly hairy for such a young guy. He has really small nipples, almost tiny. I really like small nips. I pull out my dick and start jacking off.

Why the hell not?

Rich pulled down the boy's shorts. A biggish, beautiful, nineteen-year-old cock sprang forth, boyishly ready for action. It was, somewhat surprisingly, considering age and locale, cut. Maybe the kid was Jewish.

"That feels fucking good," Bobby said, though he didn't have to. He already had his money, and it was unlikely that flattery would get him a larger tip, or—judging from what had already happened—any tip at all. But it was true.

The dark-haired guy was a good—no, a great—cocksucker. He was just as happy that the guy hadn't expected things to be the other way around. It was always hard to tell beforehand who was supposed to do what to who, not unless you asked a lot of questions, and Bobby didn't do that. A dollar was, after all, a dollar. And anyway, he really didn't mind sucking cock. Truth to tell, it was actually pretty fun, though he'd still rather be with a girl, mostly.

Rich—his mouth still on Bobby's cock, nose buried in the boy's bushy, nicely smelly pubes—moved his hand, which had been stroking the boy's muscular thigh, around to his firm, furry ass. The boy flinched, but didn't object, so Rich groped farther, till his fingertips made contact with Bobby's moist, warm asshole. The little ring pulsed, then relaxed, as though it was not unused to a bit of attention.

Nathan, meanwhile, hard-on in hand, had moved beside the bed and kind of crouched down, jockeying for a better viewpoint. Stroking himself, he watched the hustler's sizable dick disappear down Rich's throat, then reappear, then vanish again. Rich always was good at deep-throating, a knack that Nathan, with his hard-to-conquer gag reflex, envied.

Rich thought he could already taste precum, faintly salty on his tongue. But he wasn't about to let the boy shoot yet; he wanted to get his money's worth. He reluctantly backed away from Bobby's musky crotch and managed to pull the suburban boy's shorts entirely off. Rich reached down for the kid's battered high-tops and pulled the boy's legs up, revealing a very pink hole nestled in dark-blond fur. Bobby let out an *Unh!*

but was otherwise compliant. Bending down, Rich nuzzled the boy's furry balls, then ran his tongue down the kid's ridge until he could taste asshole. The boy was, as expected, musky down there, considerably funkier than his bush had been, but still not unpleasantly so. But then, Rich loved eating ass. Especially—he had to guiltily admit to himself—young ass. He licked around for a while, then burrowed his tongue up inside the boy. Bobby seemed to like the sensation. At least he squirmed and moaned as though he did, and, Rich thought, he probably wasn't all that good an actor. He propped the boy's sneakers on his shoulders and reached for Bobby's furry asscheeks, spreading them till the hole was open wide. He really wanted to get up inside there, as far up that hole as he could.

Nathan had climbed onto the motel bed, kneeling beside the boy's shaggy blond head. He wanted to fuck the nineteen-year-old's maloccluded mouth, buckteeth or no. He hovered over Bobby, rubbing his hard cock against the boy's face. Bobby did not, however, open his mouth, the way a good hustler should. If anything, he seemed to turn his face away from Nathan's dick.

"Suck my cock," Nathan said.

Bobby didn't.

Nathan repeated it, fairly snarling this time. "Suck my cock, cocksucker!"

Still no response.

Nathan hauled off and slapped Bobby's face, pretty hard.

I've still got my tongue inside the kid's ass when I hear the slap.

*Oh, Jesus,* I think, *Nathan's at it again.*

I take my mouth away from Bobby's only slightly dirty butt and look up. Nathan's kneeling on the bed, his hand poised for another blow. The kid has a look of surprise on his almost-handsome face. Not shock, just mild surprise. Not even fear. But then, he probably figures that, pitted against two aging queers, he can hold his own.

I, on the other hand, am basically miffed. This is not what I'm into, not what I had in mind. Sure, I, like Nathan, want to fuck the boy's face. I just don't want the face to be reddened and tear-stained when I fuck it. Nathan does, though, and it looks as though I'm not going to have any choice.

Nathan brings his hand down again, slapping chest this time, not face. The boy looks at me, maybe pleadingly.

"Try to relax Bobby," I say softly. "Let him do what he wants." The kid's dick is still hard.

Nathan wouldn't dare pull this kind of shit with me. Not anymore. But here? In a cheesy motel, with a teenage hustler? Yeah, sure.

Nathan hits the kid on the chest one more time, on the other tit this time. It makes a sharp *crack*.

The boy still doesn't open his mouth, though. Instead, he slides off the bed and gets on his knees. Mouth open, eyes closed.

Nathan stands up, led by his cock.

As usual.

Bobby got off the bed and got down on his knees, waiting.

Nathan positioned himself right in front of him and grabbed a shock of the boy's blond hair, pulling Bobby's head back as he slid the head of his dick into the kid's mouth. Rich watched as Nathan began fucking the boy's handsome, imperfect face. Slowly at first, then more and more brutally, furiously, slapping Bobby's face, pulling his hair. Rich probably should have found it appalling, but he didn't. It was, well yeah, exciting. He began to get that queasy feeling you get on the lift hill of a roller coaster, like you should want to get off, but you can't, so you might as well relax and enjoy it. Rich wouldn't have been able to stop Nathan even if he'd wanted to.

And he didn't want to. No, not really.

Nathan continued fucking face for a few more minutes as Bobby sputtered and drooled. Then he said, hard dick still in the kid's mouth, "Get on the bed. All fours, so I can fuck you."

As he got off his knees and got up on the bed, Bobby said, pleading, sounding suddenly more Southern, "Y'all are going to use a rubber, aren't you, mister? I got one in my pocket." He might have been suburban, but Bobby was selling country

There were some condoms in the luggage as well, but Nathan rifled through the boy's shorts and drew out a foil packet. Staring at the boy's hairy crack, he unrolled the latex over his stiff dick. Lacking proper lube, he got up a good mouthful of spit and hocked it into his hand, coating his cock. A second handful went into the boy's exposed hole, followed by a couple of Nathan's fingers.

Rich felt like he was going to come. He pulled his palm off his dick just in time.

With his free hand, Nathan began spanking the boy's butt. The first couple of slaps were met with delighted, maybe feigned, sighs, but as the blows became harder, leaving red handprints below the blond fur, Bobby's sighs ceased. If Rich had been able to see the boy's face—which he couldn't—he might have seen a grimace.

Nathan stopped the spanking and pulled out his fingers. He spit another gob into his hand, relubed his now-dry dick, and, without further ceremony, shoved the head of his cock into Bobby's loosened hole. It went inside with an amusing little pop. Nathan shoved his cock all the way in and began riding the nineteen-year-old's bought-and-paid-for ass.

*That fucking Rich. Fucking pussy Rich, with his fucking qualms. The boy wants it, can't he see the boy wants it?*

*And anyway, the kid's just some whore. Who the fuck cares what he wants?*

*Fucking pussy.*

*I mean, I love Rich, but sometimes...*

Rich, feeling like he was in a porno or else in a dream, walked around to the other side of the bed and shoved his cock in Bobby's face. The boy opened his bucktoothed mouth and Rich fucked it. He was concerned about feeling teeth—especially since Nathan's screwing had become brutally vigorous—but the kid knew what he was doing.

Rich looked over the boy's broad, young back. Nathan looked totally into it now, with an expression that someone who didn't know him might have thought psychotic. He looked back at his boyfriend and smiled. It might have been an evil grin, it might not have been. Regardless, Nathan pulled his cock out, peeled off the rubber, and plunged his dick back into the boy's loose, wet hole. Rich should have stopped him, but he didn't say a word. And when Nathan, fucking hard, spit on the boy's back, Rich felt himself losing control, and, helpless, he shot a big load down the suburban boy's throat.

Nathan must have noticed that. He, too, suddenly climaxed, pumping his load deep into Bobby's guts. For the first time in very long minutes, he lost his look of fury, his face becoming relaxed, almost vacant.

The rest was a matter of catching breaths, wiping up, and getting dressed. There was awkward small talk. Bobby made a trip to the bathroom, but didn't bother to shower. No more was said about extra cash. There was no tip.

Nathan showed the boy out the door, locking it after him. He looked over to Rich, who had an unreadable look on his face.

"What?" Nathan asked.

"Oh...nothing."

That poor guy, the one who all he wanted to do was eat my ass. When his boyfriend started slapping me around, he looked like he was gonna piss himself. What'd he think I was gonna do? Call the cops? Take on both of them? Cry?

He didn't know it, but I've had worse. Much worse. Course, I've had better, too. But a job is a job, a dollar's a dollar. And then, while he was fucking me, the redhead pulled off his rubber, like I wasn't going to know. But he was the one who didn't know. He didn't know that I've had it for a couple of years now. Maybe he'll find out.

Shit, I hope Daddy's sobered up when I get home.

A couple of days later, Nathan drove the rental car out of town, back to the Orlando airport, where they would catch a flight to L.A.

"Sorry about my family," Nathan said.

"S'okay," said Rich.

The almost-familiar places whizzed by. The back roads lined by lush old Southern growth, the streets filled with cheapjack houses accessorized with beat-up trucks.

The corner where they'd picked up the suburban boy.

The church that commanded them to Accept Jesus!

Or else.

# "fifteen minutes naked"

Jimmy Hamada

The door opens and you enter the photographer's apartment. You study him: his intriguing brown eyes, spiky hair, bearded chin. He shakes your hand and invites you into the living room. You follow him, check out his ass, rush into your explanation of why you're here after chatting with him online, a nervous swell in your stomach.

The photographer is quiet and thoughtful, putting you at ease. It's as if you've met before, but you can't remember where. He strikes up a conversation, something breezy about hooking up online. You've done it a few times yourself, but the guys rarely turn out to be what you expect.

"So what made you decide to come over?"

You feel his eyes on you, enjoy the sensation. "I dunno. I've never done this before. I've, you know, seen your work online and thought, what the fuck?"

"Then you know what I do."

"Yeah. I guess that's why I'm here too." You look at the

photographs covering the walls, dozens of guys. All white. "You never shoot Asians?" You sit on the sofa, stretch out dramatically, savoring the fact that he's watching you. "I mean, it's a potato farm in here."

"What do you mean?"

You reference the wall, the men in various poses and stages of undress. "They're all Bleach Boys."

"A boy is a boy is a boy," the photographer shrugs. "They all have mouths and cocks."

You suppress a smile, maintain your distance while your heart is running like a rabbit. "Yeah, but life needs variety. Cocks come in different colors."

He smiles charmingly. "We all come in white, last I checked." He leans back, you lean forward. "You've been to my site. You know what I look for."

"Yeah." A sigh, a confession. "Those guys are hot. Way hotter than me."

"I don't think so. Just different." The photographer studies you, like a spotlight on your fair skin. You blink rapidly, a habit left over from childhood. Laugh and cover your mouth with your hand.

"Don't do that," he says.

"What?"

"Cover your face like that." His hand straddles his face, peers between thick fingers. You wonder what those fingers will do to you.

"Why don't we go in there?" He points to a small room just off the living room. Its only furnishing is a large lamp and a mirror in the corner. You walk in, looking around like a tourist, back slowly against the wall. You pose, hooker style, with one leg crooked up behind you, foot planted on the wall; tilt your hips out, close your eyes and wait for him to approach.

He'll be eating out of your hand any second.

The photographer deflates your balloon. "No, be natural."

You drop your leg and stand against the wall, feeling like a suspect in a lineup. Thoughts of jailhouse porn movies dance through your head. You're Jeff Stryker and Brandon Lee in one package; halfway to hard already.

He remains on the threshold of the little room, tilts his head thoughtfully. "Have you ever done this before? Has someone taken pictures of you?" The camera fires.

"Not naked." A flush charges your face with color. You are suddenly too warm and slip out of your light jacket, balling it into the corner of the room. "Well...I can't believe I'm saying this, my, uh, boyfriend and I did it once. It was just for us, you know? Digital."

"And what did you do afterward?" A slow series of clicks reminds you that he's taking pictures. With actual film.

You smile, the memory flooding back. "We fucked like dogs." You look out the window down onto the avenue. Cars flash by, sun glinting off windshields. "Can they see me?"

"No one can see you except me."

The room gets warmer. You look around at the bare walls, at the platoon of men framed on the walls behind him. "So what do I do? Just stand here?"

"Do whatever you want. Whatever you are comfortable with." He raises his camera and stares through his viewfinder. "You're beautiful. Nice smile."

"You think so?" You cover your mouth with your hand, then remember his previous objection and pull it away, stare deep into the camera, look stern.

"Doesn't your boyfriend think so? Don't you?"

"I guess so. He doesn't, you know, say anything about me being beautiful."

"He should. Look at yourself in the mirror. What do you see?"

You move closer to the rectangular mirror, stare at the boy framed in it, like the boys on the wall in the other room. You don't recognize him, have to look past the outfit you'd so carefully orchestrated only an hour ago. You ask this boy if he's ready for this. He nods enthusiastically.

"Tell me what you see."

You laugh uncomfortably, then stare back at your own brown eyes. "Brown eyes. I hate them."

"Why?"

"So common. Everyone has brown eyes. I wish they were blue."

The photographer moves the camera away from his face. You notice that he's got eyes just as deep and brown as your own. You shrug, but gloat internally, return to your reflection. "I dunno. A boy. Dark shaggy hair. He's skinny…too small. Like a bird."

"Like a boy." The photographer fires off a few more shots. You figure he knows what he's talking about. "That's what I like about the Japanese. You will always look like a boy."

"Pedophile." You smile at him, then turn it back on the guy in the mirror. He's not bad. If you did rice, you'd fuck him.

"Why don't you take off your shoes? Relax." He drops the camera and watches you from six feet away. You wish he would move closer.

"Trying to get me naked?" You squat and untie your sneakers, fumbling to arrange your hard-on without him noticing. Flushing from your neck up, like fireworks.

"That's what we're here for." He smiles abstractly.

You slip off your sneakers, tuck the socks within; place your sneakers to the side of the room, out of the shot. You wonder if your feet smell. You return to the window and watch the light play across the cars, enjoying the warm wood beneath your naked feet.

"Would you like it if the people on the street could see you?" The gentle click of the camera counts off a series of shots.

"I dunno." You tilt your head into the glass, stare down at the pedestrians, imagine yourself naked on the fire escape outside. "Maybe. I might like it."

"You should."

You turn back to him, stare into the big eye of the camera, feel the heat of its attention. "So," clearing your throat, "what would you like me to do?"

"What do you want to do?" *Click*. Pause. The camera loads the film with a mechanical whirr.

"Uh..." You laugh. "Get naked and fuck, I guess. Yeah, I could do that."

"Why don't you start with the shirt?"

You lift your polo shirt, baring your thin torso and the sprinkle of hair around your belly button. You ease it over your head as the steady pulse of the camera fills the room. You toss your shirt at him with a warm smile. "Aren't you getting naked too?"

"Why don't you stand over there, by the lamp." You saunter over to the tall lamp with the globe top and prop yourself next to it. You undo the top button of your jeans, exposing the waistband of your briefs, thrust your hips forward. You study him as he shoots you, his face intense and focused. You smile. His jeans are tenting but he keeps his distance.

You clear your throat, pause, afraid of distracting him. "So, like, how many guys have you shot? Like this?"

"A few." He sounds distant. The photographer moves closer, you tilt into his approach. "Look at me. Give me your eyes."

You stare into the camera, eyes wide and hopeful. You wet your lips and pout like you've seen in the porn movies, but he reminds you to be natural. He makes a joke about your obvious erection and you laugh. A volley of shots capture your image. "Good, that's what I want."

You run your hands down your chest, stopping to finger a nipple, then graze the waistband of your jeans. "You want me to take these off?"

"Whatever you feel comfortable with." He reloads the camera; the soft whirr of film fills the silence.

You toy with your jeans, not sure if you are ready, but your hands are already moving full speed ahead. You edge the denim down your thighs, letting it pool at your ankles. The camera clicks. You step out of your jeans on unsteady feet, falling against the wall as you stumble. Red stripes flush your cheeks. "Duh!"

Your white briefs barely cover you, your dick is straining the fabric. You realign your erection, making it diagonal against your pelvis. You look in the mirror, watch yourself being photographed, constantly aware of the man watching you.

"That's nice."

A few more shots click off as your cock inches up and out of the waistband. You finger the head and flick the precum off the slit. You turn around, inching your briefs down to expose the soft mound of your ass. "You like it?"

The camera agrees with a series of clicks. "Turn around," he says. His voice is deep and commanding. You comply, covering your erection. You stare down at your body, memories of beating off burning in your head. You're not naked, but feel exposed, raw, excited.

You pull down the front of your briefs, trapping your thighs with the fabric. Your cock springs into your hand and you keep it covered, feeling its heat singe your palm. "Move your hand," he says. You stand with your back against the wall, dropping your hands to your sides, a dare in your eyes.

He moves into the room with you, the only sounds your comingled breath, the soft click of the camera marking thrumming seconds. You step out of your briefs, spread your legs, expose yourself.

The whirr of the camera announces the end of the roll. "Okay, I think we're done."

You wait for something else to happen, your dick begging for it. The photographer steps back into the living room, putting the rolls of film into black canisters, his camera back into the back. You wait for something to happen, really need it to. "I uh...I thought we were going to..."

"It's okay. Get dressed and we can schedule another shoot. You've got great architecture."

You stroke your cock, look at him longingly. He watches. "I need to, you know."

He nods, keeps his eyes on you. You stroke yourself, moving to the center of the room, bridging the distance, one, two, three steps; a drizzle of precum puddles on the floor. You slick the head of your cock, watch him watching you, having never jerked off in front of a complete stranger before, your skin singing with his attention. "You want to help me?" A froggy-throated request.

"You are doing fine on your own." He sits in the chair as you turn to the mirror, look at that boy in the mirror, the lean tight boy with the shaggy hair, pumping his cock, inching himself quickly, tweaking a nipple and biting down on his lip, jerking off to you. You explode, pounding yourself into submission, legs weak, mouth dry, heaving sperm onto the floor and the mirror.

A tense silence, broken only by your breath, the traffic outside, a jackhammer in the distance. "See, I told you it was white," he says, pointing at the river of sperm sliding down the mirror. He hands you a towel and you clean off, slip into your clothes while he watches.

"Email me and we'll set up another session." Back to business. He escorts you back to the door, barely an hour in, encouraging you to come back for the second round, telling you that the proofs from today will be ready by then. You'll get a free print, your choice. You can barely hear him, your body zinging in a hundred directions. You bound back out into the day, thinking of surprising your boyfriend at work, and fucking him into next week. Hell no, fucking him all week.

# A BEAUTIFUL FACE

Robert Patrick

At eighteen, I was a little backward even by the standards of a small Midwest American town in 1950. I had never cum with anyone, even though I sometimes thought I heard my cousins jacking off in the dark at the same time as I did when family gatherings caused us to bed down together. Chester, my best friend in high school—well, really, I guess, my only friend anywhere, ever—Chester, who was lean and lanky and had straight, greasy hair, said he hung around with me only "because beautiful people have more fun." I never even thought about what he might have meant by that. Or we could just leave it that I never thought. It never seemed to me that I had any fun for him to share, unless the group picnics, school dances, and chorus and glee club activities I got bullied into doing were his idea of fun. I guess they were.

Came graduation, Chester declared that he was going to go to Hollywood and be an actor. Well, he did go to Hollywood. I got a crumpled postcard with someone's footprints on it, saying,

*You ought to come visit me sometime.*

Not long after, a girl from my class whom I had asked to the graduation dance but hadn't kissed went pretty crazy and told people I was the devil. They dragged her away, but my folks put me on a Greyhound bus with a hundred dollars and a small valise and said maybe I'd be happier there, I should look it over. I wasn't aware that I seemed unhappy. I wasn't aware of anything. In retrospect, I suppose I was a bit of a zombie. Good grades, good hygiene, and, as I realize now, good looks, but nothing happening whatsoever.

The greatest novelty of the two-day trip to Hollywood was that I got off the bus smelly and dirty. I don't think I'd ever actually been dirty before. Chester met me at the station, looking weirdly spiffed-up, his greasy hair arranged in a kind of upsweep, and he wore a leather jacket. He had a car that clanked and grunted and groaned as he took us up into some hills behind Grauman's Chinese Theatre to what I now realize was a slum, but the palm trees and sunshine and the fact the house was pink made me feel I was in Oz.

I was surprised that the single back room he rented had only a screen door, not a wooden one. But its lack of any furniture but a mattress covered with a single sheet seemed romantic and Bohemian, like the beatniks I had vaguely read about. We were no sooner inside than he started touching me and asking how I felt. Before very long he had our pants down and lay on top of me on the mattress and rubbed our cocks together till we came, while I watched a tiny airplane in the chalk-blue sky through the tattered door-screen.

I was thrilled and trembling. I just wanted to do it again, but he made us toasted cheese sandwiches on a waffle iron and went on and on about an audition he had, a "cattle call" for young men. That night he huffed and gasped on top of me twice more with my enthusiastic approval. In the morning he told me to come with him. I would have leapt into the sun if he told me to.

We clunked to a several-story white stucco building and went upstairs to a way-sunny room with a polished floor (probably, now that I reflect on it, a dance studio) where a hundred guys our age, mostly dressed like Chester, stood multiplied by big mirrors. I was thinking only of what we had done last night and wondering how many times we would do it when we left this place. We were given numbers and stood watching as the boys in pairs read some lines from wrinkled script pages. I think I dimly wondered what it might be like to do it with some of the other boys, but that may be my current old man's fantasies interfering with memory. Anyway, at a long table sat several men and women who took notes and sometimes asked a few questions of a boy. But most boys were stopped after a few lines and told, "Thank you."

When they called Chester's number, he dragged me forward with him and handed me pages. I read whatever the pages said in between his speeches. I really don't remember what it was. Halfway through the short scene, there was a whistle. I looked up and saw a tall man in a gray suit leaning in a far corner, hard to see clearly because of the sun. He made a little figure-eight with one finger and a woman at the table said to us, "Switch parts, please." Chester started the scene again, reading what I had read before. I read what had been his lines. We were allowed to read the whole scene.

The lady called us to the table and asked a few questions (birthday, birthplace, experience), always glancing at the man in the corner. She asked me to stay. Chester looked bewildered, depressed. He trickled out, saying he'd wait outside. The man in the corner waved his hand slightly, and a man at the table went out just behind Chester.

The man in the suit walked out. Another man from the table took my arm and walked me out. On the sidewalk, the first table-man was talking to Chester and giving him money. Chester kept looking quickly from the money in the man's hands, up to me, then back at the money. I was shown into a limousine where the man in gray waited, smiling.

As we rode out to Malibu, he asked me many questions about my life. Somewhere amongst them, he told me that he was the producer of "the picture," and that I should call him Carter. The car stopped at what looked like a pretty plain little house, but when we went through the front door, the interior was revealed to be huge and dark and round, until your eyes got used to the soft light coming through seaside walls of curved, tinted glass.

We sat on enormous cushions on the floor by an unlit fireplace. Quiet servants brought us cool drinks and later a light dinner, as he discussed "the picture" and "the role." I hadn't the slightest idea what he was talking about, but the soft carpet, the sideways sun across the sea, the susurrating sounds of the tinted waves and the wind, and the smell and taste of the excellent, unknown food were mesmerizing. He said I'd stay there for the night. And excused himself.

An Asian servant who was already in hat and coat to leave showed me to a vast, nearly empty bedroom, and left. The bed was triple-size and round, raised on two round step-levels. I sat on it and saw myself reflected in a big dressing-table mirror. There was nothing on the table.

Carter came in in a dressing gown over pajamas. "My wife's room," he said. "She left me just lately." He came up the steps, undressed me, and laid me back on the bed, my lower legs over the edge. He spread my legs and knelt on the top step. With a nervous smile at me, he bent his head down and sucked my cock.

The last light of the setting sun shone on his small bald spot. I got hard in his hot wetness very soon, and shot a wad that came spewing back out of his mouth. He looked up, white cream on his chin, then lifted my legs and very slowly forced his dick into my asshole. It felt very odd and I hardly recognized it as sex, but he took my hand, placed it on my sticky dick, and made motions with it. I jacked and soon became erect again, and the getting fucked became quite pleasant. He whispered for me to cum, so I did, and then, I suppose, he did. He pulled out of me and stood staring down at my asshole, which must have been a mess, for some time. His hand almost went out to touch it, but he spun and left instead.

The next day one car showed up with my sparse luggage, and others showed up with teachers and designers and photographers and press-persons. They took photos, then dyed my hair and took more photos, then threw the first photos away and changed my clothes and took my picture again. The woman who had been at the audition table came, too, and talked with Carter a lot in corners. He got a bit gruff and red-faced and she got quiet and nodded. She stood in the corner still nodding, even when he walked away from her and came toward me, smiling, asking, "And how's our boy? How's our golden boy?"

Each day the director of the picture came by and worked with me on the script. It seemed I was to play a boy who raised a favorite horse, only to have it die at the very finish of a great race. There was dispute about its position at the finish line, but ultimately it was decided that the little unknown horse had won. There was an inconclusive adolescent love story, too.

Each day I studied the script and diction, and exercised with a Swedish man. A tall blond man taught me riding along the beach. And each night Carter came into my room and sputtered my white goo onto his chin and my thighs, then pushed prick in and out of me till I blew my second load and he his first. And each night he lingered looking down at the load seeping from my excited anus.

I wasn't aware that my anus had become excited until one afternoon an Asian came down onto the beach and told my riding master that Mister Carter would not be in until very, very late. To my surprise, I thought, "He may not fuck me tonight!" and my anus squeezed and squeezed and throbbed like some kind of bizarre hollow cock while my real, external cock got semihard in my jodhpurs.

I don't know how the riding instructor knew he could fuck me. He told me years later that he "could smell it." Anyway, he threw me back on the bed and jammed joint in me, without blowing me and without asking any permission. His cock was longer than Carter's, but I missed the blow job and came too soon, so it was annoying to have him keep fucking me while I pulled at my own soft, mucky meat.

But Carter appeared in the bedroom doorway and stood there wide eyed. The riding instructor saw where my gaze went and turned to see his boss. He just grinned and shrugged and kept on fucking me. Carter stood staring. I sat up on my elbows and saw in the wife's mirror the riding instructor's ass, its hairy hole snapping each time he drove dick into me. I suppose that was what Carter saw, too.

The blond finished in me, pulled out with flair, and walked down the steps, grabbing his clothes casually. At the door, he made a lordly gesture to Carter, meaning, *Please feel free to use the facilities now.*

Carter came over to the bed and up the steps. He stood looking down at whatever was leaking out of me. He knelt, I thought to blow me. But he stayed still for a long time, and then dipped his head down and started sucking my asshole.

I gasped and buckled and twisted, but his hands gripped my knees. I saw stars and clouds and went in and out of consciousness. In one moment of awareness, I saw that my legs were around his neck holding his face in my flue, and I was aware that I was grinding my gut-end against his slurping, moaning mouth.

I forced my eyes to focus in the gloom and saw his face rise for breath from between my thighs. Never had I seen anything like it. His forehead and cheeks shone with cum and sweat and spit. It was like sunrise. His eyes were blurry like mine, but seemed to be looking at something supernatural. His mouth was stretched in a smile I'd never seen even in paintings of saints. He stared at me, past me, into me for a moment, and then went back in there for more of whatever he was experiencing in my ass.

I got hard and jacked until I shot vulgarly, abundantly on myself. Without a thought I shoved the load down, down past my balls to flavor my anus for him. I think he jacked off a couple of times, too. Anyway, he made orgasmic noises.

Then he left me. Next morning, all sorts of people woke me to tell me that he had asphyxiated himself in the garage. The woman I recognized said he had left me the house, and his wife wouldn't contest it because she got two others, and anyway there was blackmail on her, but I'd be a fool to keep it, because I'd never be able to afford the upkeep unless this picture was an unprecedented hit.

Making the movie was easy. Carter had told the press I was perfect for the part and really, he was right. All I had to do was show up and say my lines. The professional actors were very kind to me.

But they couldn't help on the last day of shooting when the director three times threw his script down and left the set and had to be sweet-talked back. The movie ended with a close-up for my character, his reaction after weeks of total despair to hearing that the brave little horse had indeed won the race of its life. I made every face I could think of, but nothing pleased the director. He screamed to a studio official right on the set, "The script is thin and dry, all the way. Everything hangs on this moment. I can light the little lout, I can bring up music from every side, but if he can't show us complicated joy, we're down the fucking drain." That was extreme. Back in 1950, people didn't casually say "fucking" in public.

Everyone was avoiding looking at me where I sat in overalls on a hay bale. I felt pretty bad. I thought of Chester and the Asian servants. And my folks and schoolmates back home, who must be pretty excited about all of this. And I thought of the house, that great, sprawling, beautiful thing on the beach. I thought of sunlight, sunset light, night-light reflected from the sea and sky.

And all of a sudden I saw something else. I shouted at the director, "Do you think we could try one more take?" and he sighed and signaled for silence, sound, speed, action.

And I imitated Carter's face rising between my legs, beaming from its first feast of asshole and cum and utter degradation and total fulfillment, and, well, just look where I am today.

# WE MESSED AROUND AT THE EL CAMINO MOTEL

Shane Allison

I was watching a rerun of "ER" when the phone rang.

"Shane, telephone!" Ma yelled.

I sat my dinner of soggy cornflakes and bananas next to the TV remote on the bedside table.

"Hang it up!" I hollered. "Hello?"

"Wa'sup?" asked the soft but brazen voice on the other end. It was Chris.

"Hey, whatchoo doin'?"

"I have two hours until Ciara comes back, if you want to come over." His words made my gut tingle with excitement.

"Mkay. U'm leavin' now."

"How long will it take you t' get here?"

"Gimme 'bout fifteen minutes."

"Hurry up," said Chris.

I slipped on my shoes, poured the bowl of breakfast cereal into the toilet, grabbed my keys, and told Ma that someone had called from the library to tell me that I'd left my wallet.

"Dey closed," she said.

"Not th' campus library. Dey open 'til two," I told her. I couldn't get out of the house fast enough.

*Shit, this is it*, I thought. I hauled ass out of the driveway. I was minutes away from having Chris's dick in my mouth, from inhaling his musky scent. It had been months since we last messed around. Chris said we had to take shit easy after we came close to getting caught by Ciara. I haven't made things easy by blowing up his cell every two minutes, and bombarding him with endless text messages. Things are complicated with him and Ciara. He keeps me around for the occasional fuck-and-suck session.

I drove as fast as Ma's Taurus could take. My dick stretched and stiffened in my jeans as images of reaming Chris's ass danced in my head. The sick sensation I often get right before I'm about to get fucked hit me. I rubbed my belly and the feeling subsided.

I was three stoplights away from having my face fucked. I couldn't believe that Ciara had gone out—she's always under Chris, more than ever since he moved out of his crib on Chapel Drive.

Chris had had enough of his deadbeat landlord's bullshit about replacing the carpet in the apartment, soaked by a busted toilet. It turned out every shitter in the apartment complex had backed up. Chris refused to pay one red cent of rent until the toilet was fixed and the mildewed carpet was removed. The landlord threatened to sue. Chris moved out, and who the hell could blame him? I wouldn't have paid their asses either if I had to walk around on shitty wet carpet.

Chris relocated to the El Camino Motel, sandwiched between his old place and his job. Shit wasn't the Hilton, but it was cheap. Chris was paying by the week. A few days after he moved in,

Ciara quit her job at Hip-Hop Fish and Chicken, and couldn't make the rent so she, too, had to get to steppin'. Now she and Chris are living out of this roach-infested dive until he can get up enough money for a down payment on a new crib. When I recommended that he get the money from his folks, he looked like he wanted to stab me in the heart with a rusty shrimp fork. I don't see why not. They're loaded, living way out there in Ox Bottom Manor. A few hundred bucks to them is bubble gum change. But I get that Chris wants to do shit on his own. He's not one of these spoiled fucks who expect Daddy to bail him out of scrapes and jams.

I pulled into the lot directly in front of the motel. I knocked on the door, but he didn't answer. I peered through the verticals that hung over the window. The table and twin beds were strewn with blue Wal-Mart bags and a mixture of Southpole T-shirts and bras. The TV was on, along with a light in the bathroom. I knocked again, harder and louder. He walked shirtless out of the bathroom with a towel wrapped around his thirty-two-inch waist. Water trickled down his torso. He saw me at the window.

"Wa'sup?" he said. "I was in th' shower."

The motel smelled like toe-jam and pork dumplings. Everything he had decided not to put in storage was stacked on the floor, sitting on the beds, leaning in corners.

"So wherejoo say Ciara at?" I asked, closing the door behind me.

"At th' movies," said Chris. "Her an' 'er sister goin' out t' eat afterward."

The last time Chris and I were alone was at his apartment. If it wasn't for the sliding glass door in his bedroom leading out to the back, Ciara would have caught our asses for sure. My ass was stuffed with his butter-slathered dick when she came knocking. Ain't no telling what she would have done had she caught us. Chris don't know how crazy black women get over their men. Believe me, I know. I can't count how many times I saw Ma pull a gun on Daddy when I was growing up.

"I'll beat th' skin off ya if I eva catchchoo playin' wit this gun," I remember her telling me.

It's been hard to get Chris to even go out with me for ice cream without his ass worrying about getting caught by Ciara—who, in my opinion, ain't worth the drama. I figured she wasn't giving up no pussy if he was calling me, 'cause he never calls me for shit unless he needs money or his dick sucked. But I don't really have a problem with it. Boy's got his needs, you know?

I noticed four six-packs of Heineken and two bottles of Crown Royal on the dresser. If there was one thing his ass wasn't going to put in storage, it was his liquor.

"Hey, can I have a beer?" I asked.

Chris didn't answer. He couldn't hear me over the sizzle of the shower, so I helped myself to one. I grimaced when the lukewarm liquid flooded my mouth, but it was what I needed to soothe my nervous belly. I wondered if he had some weed. I walked to the bathroom doorway. His stark nakedness was barely visible behind the glazed shower curtain. I flashed on how funny it would be to reenact the shower scene from *Psycho*, so I snatched the tube of Aqua-Fresh from the sink and crept slowly toward Chris. The tile floor was slippery, and the bathroom mirror was fogged. I brushed back the curtain and stabbed down at Chris, screaming. He shrieked before grabbing the toothpaste.

"Man, what th' hell you doin'?"

"I wanted t' know if yo ass brought th' weed." I laughed.

"Yeah, I put it in a cookie canister. Check under th' bed over by th' window."

I peeked at his wet dick. "Lookin' good."

"Fuck you," he said, grinning, and slid the shower curtain closed.

I stepped over garbage bags to the bed and pulled out a canister that used to hold sugar and butter cookies. Chris had already rolled several doobies. I lit the blunt with a lighter sitting next to an ashtray full of cigarette butts. After three drags, I felt a buzz. The TV was showing some old episode of "A Different World." Chris was into cheesy sitcoms. I stumbled back toward the bathroom and studied Chris's burnished shape through the curtain.

He treated me sometimes like I was just one of the guys in a locker room, or a lover he had been with for many years.

"Can I join you?" I hollered.

"What?" he asked, pulling at the shower curtain.

"Can I step in there wit'choo?"

"Come on."

Normally he would have said no, cutting short any attempt to get in his pants. I got that feeling in my gut again, as I sat on the toilet to untie my boots, kick them off, and fork off my socks. I pulled off my shirt and dropped it to the damp bathroom floor. I stepped out of my jeans and kicked them into a corner. I slid back the curtain, revealing Chris's nude brawn. He was washing under his pits. Thick, white lather slipped off every beautiful part of his Catholic body and rolled into the deep ditch of his ass. I joined him under the steaming hot water, wrapping my fat arms around him as if I were his boyfriend. I played with his nipples before slipping my hand into his palm, taking the bar of soap. I lathered the waves of thick, black hair on his back. I traced along his spine with the soap, into the crack of his butt, then washed his chest and firm stomach. I adored how the lather highlighted his root beer–colored pubes. Soft, Chris was hung like a fucking donkey. Hard, his dick defied gravity.

Pearls of water dripped from his pink dickhead. I got down on bended knee like I was about to propose and took his dick into my mouth. My lips slid slippery down his stuff as the water thrashed my face.

I squeezed his nuts. I blew him, backed off, then sucked Chris's balls, a mouthful of tender scrotal skin.

The warm water was turning cold.

"Let's get out. My hands are startin' to prune," said Chris. I didn't want to stop. I could have held his dick in my mouth all night. He turned off the shower and we stepped out. I took the oversize beach towel that Chris had wrapped around himself earlier, and toweled us dry before we moved to his unmade bed, a tangle of ugly green orchid-printed sheets. Chris sat, his hefty dick hanging over the bed's edge.

"Slide back a li'l bit," I told him. I positioned myself between his thighs and took up where I left off. He tasted of clean deodorant soap. I looked into his piercing hazels as I sucked him sensuously—and slowly so my jaw muscles wouldn't tire out. I alternated from his dick to his balls and back to his dick, until he said, "I wanna fuck you." I'm more of a top, but to Chris I'm a nelly bottom. First time he used my butt, it was hella painful, but he got his dick in. All of it. Loads of lube helped.

"Where ya keep th' lotion at?" I asked.

"There should be some in the bathroom."

I searched under the bathroom sink.

"Here go some," I said. *For extra-dry skin.* I squeezed it on my fingers, reached between my asscheeks and slathered the cocoa butter–scented cream inside my hole. Chris toyed with his dick as he watched me work the lotion in. When I had applied enough, I handed the tube to Chris, and he rubbed a handful onto his dick. I assumed Chris's preferred position for me, on my back. He likes to look into my eyes while he's fucking me. I pulled back my legs as he stretched my asshole for his dick. He was so gentle.

We didn't bother with rubbers. Chris always pulled out before the money shot. I always used a condom with the Republican husbands, the nervous fiancés, and the kinky granddaddies, but I trusted Chris. He pushed inside me, inch after inch. I grasped the flowered bedspread through the discomfort. He gripped my ankles and pushed my feet against the wall behind us. My limbs ached. I watched him thrusting in the dresser mirror behind him.

"Fuck me slow," I said. I liked it when he took his time. I jacked off as he worked my butt. Chris stopped, pulled out, and applied more lotion when he dried up. Still hard, he was back inside me in seconds. I lay wondering, *Is this how you fuck Ciara? Do you fuck her better than you fuck me? Is the bitch even into back door action?* Chris took my butt on a mission. He fucked me like a porn star on cooked rock.

His dick up my butt felt like a rocket. A day don't go by that I don't wish he would dump Ciara for me, but what are you going to do with a guy that loves coochie more than cock? I'll never be nothing more than a booty call for him to fuck in seedy motels whenever Ciara's out of town or at the movies. Thing is, I've fallen in love with his ass. And don't think I haven't told him how I feel. He shrugs it off like he don't know what to say. I've said it again and again in letters and funny greeting cards, but he just smiles sweetly at my supplications. Guess that's what I get for liking a guy I met in the dirty arcade of an adult video store.

Chris was really going at me when we heard an angry knock at the door. He frantically pulled out, without warning, and leapt out of bed. My ass throbbed after his abrupt exit. He swiped a pair of boxers draped over the back of a chair and made himself decent.

"Open th' fuckin' door, Chris! I can see ya'll asses through th' blinds, so ya might as well open th' mothafuckin' door." It was Ciara.

"I thoughtchoo said she wuz go'n be gone fuh two hours?" I squawked.

She kept banging. I wrapped a towel around myself and hopped into the bathroom. There was no sliding glass door to escape through. I was trapped.

"I see yo ass!" she yelled.

Chris had no choice but to let her in. From behind the locked bathroom door, I heard her cursing like Richard Pryor.

"I know it would only be a matta o' time befo' I caughtchoo ass!"

"We weren't doin' nothin'," Chris said.

"How you go'n say you wutton doin' nothin' when U'm watchin' you fuck him?" She directed her fury at me. "Why you hidin' huh?" she screamed, banging on the bathroom door. "Yo' faggot ass!"

She turned back to Chris. "Don't touch me," she hollered. "You fuckin' nasty."

"Hol' up," he said.

"Fuck you, Chris."

I heard the door slam. I crept out , sweating. Chris pulled on jeans and a shirt, then knotted the laces of his Air Jordans.

"You all right?" I asked.

"U'm gonna go after her."

"An' say what, an' do what, man? She mad an' ain't no tellin' what she might do. Won'tchoo jus' call 'er in th' mornin'?"

"You should take off. I'll call you tomorrow," said Chris.

"C'mon, man."

"Just close th' door when you leave."

The headlights of his PT Cruiser burned my eyes as he backed out of the lot.

Chris didn't call the next day. I phoned him again and again, but his cell kept going to voice mail. I checked by the motel, but there was no sign of him. I went to Lane 7, where he worked, and sure enough, there he was. I was hesitant to walk in, thinking he would blame me for what happened, but I had to know if he had talked to her. The bowling alley wasn't busy. Chris didn't look happy to see me.

"Hey, what happened? Didjoo talk t' 'er?"

"I went to 'er cousin's house. She said Ciara wasn't there, didn't know where she spent the night. I been callin' 'er cell all day, but she won't pick up."

"Man, U'm sorry," I said, but I wasn't really. This the kinda shit that happens when you on the D.L. I thought that maybe, with her out of the picture, there was a chance for me.

"We just need to take it easy for a while until I can get 'er calmed down," he said.

I told Chris that I would give him as much time as he needed.

"Well, let me go. I gotta do inventory," said Chris.

"Gimme a call. Lemme know how things work out, an' if ya need anything, ya know what t' do."

I drove home. Life was as shitty for me as before our short-lived fuck. Who knows how long it'll be before we can get together again. More weeks and months of my ass waiting in the wings, no doubt.

# CELL 13

Tommy Lee "Doc" Boggs

Eight-by-ten, light-aquamarine walls of concrete block, two metal bunks with three-inch-thick cotton mats. One tattooed, shaved-headed convict: me. And one pretty-assed nineteen-year-old boy.

The boy thinks he's bi. I know I'm gay. He lightly flirts, I flat-out describe in detail all I want to do to him. He resists, saying he has never been with a man, only a TG girl. I sniff his dirty socks and lick his shit-stained boxers, watching him sleep while I masturbate.

When he's awake, I try every angle to get at his cock. He claims to be a top. I'm definitely a bottom. He teases me with shows of his meat. "Hey, celly, do you think I should trim this?" he asks, one hand playing with his pubes, the other hand holding his half-hard cock, precum glistening sweetly at his pee hole.

"No, it's fine. But you seem to be leaking," I tell him. "May I please clean it up?" He looks at his fully hard rod, looks back at me, shrugs, steps toward me. I lean down from where I'm sitting and gingerly lap up his precious juice. I so want to taste his whole cock, but as I begin to slide it into my trembling mouth he steps back. "No, no, no, I never said you could have it all," he says.

Damn, is he fucking with me? Angry, hurt, hungry, I cry, "What? Not fair! I want it."

"What's in it for me?" says the greedy little fuck.

"How about I draw whatever you want?" I offer. I'm an accomplished artist. Well, accomplished for a convict who has spent twenty years in state prisons, currently San Quentin. And the greedy boy has been after me for a drawing as much as I've been after his meat. But being the shrewd barterer that I am, I continued to refuse monetary payment for my craft, knowing, hoping, that someday this scenario would arise. Now's my chance.

"Ooookay," says greedy. "Let's talk turkey. One of your drawings for what, exactly? Be specific."

Finally! "For one of my bestest drawings ever, I want..." Suddenly, I can't decide: I want to smell, taste, lick, kiss his pretty boy meat, I want to swish his juice in my mouth, but...I also want to feel every inch of his cock in my hungry ass, I want his balls slapping against mine, his hot breath tickling the back of my bald head, and most of all, I want to feel him shoot his load deep into my hole. I would also love—am in fact driven quite senseless with the thought of doing so—to tongue-fuck his pink hole; lick his sweaty, slightly calloused toes; bury my nose in his soft downy armpit and inhale his young, musky scent. But I must negotiate cautiously lest he become aware of my barely controlled desire. I decide: "I want to suck your dick till you cum in my mouth."

He pretends to agonize, though we both know it's just an act to allow him to feel like he's won, like it was all really my idea and he is not gay. *Right.* In the end, he says, "Deal. You draw me a picture of Supergirl and I will cum in your mouth." Silly kid. I own his punk ass now.

Time to hammer out the details, the when where what. We're in county lockup. The front of the cell is all glass, and so are all of the surrounding cells. The guards make bi-hourly circuits to ensure they have the correct number of breathing bodies, which is a concern for us, but only a minor one. Also, the cells are open from nine in the morning to nine in the evening, and we can come and go to the showers, find a book, watch TV, phone someone, whatever. I may be totally gay, but I'm also totally closeted, which causes me to be extremely cautious when getting it on. So here's what we decide: tonight, as soon as we lock up at nine P.M. and the guard does his final circuit before the changing of the watch, we'll do it.

All day the tension rises, my cock as well, as I fantasize about this evening's festivities. We hardly say two words to each other, but I catch him watching me watch him watch me. Whew!

Around eight-thirty, t-minus thirty, I see greedy boy preparing to shower. Oh, no! Can't have that. I want him *au naturale*. I head him off, standing naked to the waist in cell 13. "Hey dude, you're not going to fuckin' believe this. No hot water. Fuck, typical bullshit,"

"What?" He looks stricken. "But what about tonight? I hafta shower or we can't..." His distress is obvious.

"No, no, no, don't trip, bud, we're still on," I explain. "You took one yesterday, no biggie."

"Are you sure? I can smell my balls, man." At that, my knees go weak and I collapse into our single chair, cock quivering, mind racing with thoughts of his smelly balls bouncing off my stubbly chin, resting on my tongue. *Don't you worry, my pretty little punk, I will leave them smelling fresh and clean!* "No problem. I don't mind," I say.

He shrugs and gets dressed. Never does he question my statement concerning our hot water supply, nor does it seem to occur to him that in all of recorded history these showers have not had sizzling hot water. I wonder who's fooling whom?

Showtime! The guard calls for us to "Lock it up, ladies." We hustle to our cells. As I close the door to 13, my boy is lying on his back, book in hand, pretending to read, with a rather large, obvious tent under the covers. I turn off the light and hang my blanket off the top bunk, veiling his lower bunk. "Hey, what do you think you're doing?"

I look at him, eyes large, heart sinking. "I'm putting up a curtain so we don't get caught," I explain.

"Who said I was ready?" he challenges.

I lose it. "Fuck it then, I mean, you get a blow job dude, I have to pay for it, that's a win-win for you, so, whatever, I'll just go to bed." I turn the light back on and begin to remake my bed as he says, "Only kidding, god! Don't be so touchy. Let's do it."

"No, fuck, I don't want you to do anything you don't want to. I want you to want it and enjoy it, not just do it for a reward," I complain, falsely, hoping to the gods that I'm reading him right.

"So, I'm not going to get my drawing?" he whines.

"No, I'll do your drawing." I climb to my bunk.

"Thanks," he mumbles.

Ten minutes later, I hear, "Hey, um, what if I said I wanted to?" That was the longest ten minutes of my life. I was afraid I had overplayed my hand. "Well, what exactly do you want to do?"

He says, "What we talked about." Still timid. How cute.

"You mean I can suck your cock?" I ask. I look over the edge of my bunk, down at him. He is uncovered to just below his waist, knees up, hands under the covers. "Let me see it." He slowly, shyly pulls his long, thin, pink cock out. It's beautiful. A little small, but who cares. He's nineteen and adorable.

"Will you fuck me?" I ask.

"What? No way," he blusters, and stashes his pretty cock back under the covers. I almost cry. "Sorry, okay, no big deal," I say as I scramble off my bunk to kill the light. After I'm down, I notice the guard is gone. Perfect! I put up the curtain and grab his boxers without another word. He covers his eyes with his forearm, face expressionless. I pull the boxers down. They catch on his softly fuzzy asscheeks. He arches slightly to accommodate me as I slip them across his butt, down his thighs and calves and over his size-eleven feet. I sniff his toes, kiss the tip of each one softly, fearing a bad reaction. Nothing. My cock is fat, hard, throbbing, leaking precum. I spread his ankles, slide my hands up his calves, over his knees, over his thighs. I rub my face up his leg to his fat sac, nuzzle his balls, lick them, smell them. It's almost too much, I cum some. I have to slow down. I want this to last. I take his shaft in my hand and he pees a little squirt. I lick it up, suck it dry. I lick his salty taint, tongue his hole, move to his cock. He's bigger than I first thought. But I'm a deep-throat specialist. I slip his slender cock down my gullet with one thrust. I slobber on his meat till he whispers—much to my surprise and delight—"Do you still want me to fuck you?"

Without a word, I jump up, grab the petroleum jelly, lube my throbbing, impatient hole, and spread more lube on his hard cock.

"How do we do it? I've never fucked a man before," he whispers again. *Wow.* "However you want," I say. "My favorite is doggie-style. But when you cum, please tell me so I can turn around and take your load in my mouth."

I get into position, face in the pillow, arms out, knees drawn up to my chest, ass high in the air. He's a first-timer, and he treats my ass like a pussy, slamming straight home. I gasp and squirt cum, lots of cum. "Want me to stop?" he asks. I can't speak, so I shake my head no, wiping the tears off on his pillow, and push my ass toward him. He gets the idea and slides his cock out till just the tip rests against my hurt hole, then this time pushes in more slowly, more gently, inch by inch past my swollen prostate, in and then out again, slowly building speed till I'm having trouble breathing, till he suddenly shoves my ass hard with his hands. "Now, now, now, I'm going to cum!" He strokes his cock rapidly and I lunge for it and he explodes a fat hot sweet stream of cum into my hungry mouth. I suck and slurp all he's willing to feed me, and then some. I finish by cleaning my own shit and blood from his cock and balls.

"Wow," says my pretty little punk, smiling sheepishly. "Who would've guessed? It was way great."

I simply smile, sweetly kiss his still-hard cock, and quietly go to bed.

# BETTER LATE THAN NEVER

Rachel Kramer Bussel

After I got divorced, I resigned myself to a fairly lonely existence. Well, not entirely lonely, but sexless, certainly. Even before the breakup, Stella and I had become little more than roommates, and the truth was, though we had managed to get it on occasionally, I was never all that into it, so this seemed like the usual state of affairs for me, except now I was living alone. At thirty-seven, I wasn't fresh meat, but I wasn't totally over the hill. Friends, many of whom came out of the woodwork after the split, tried to set me up on blind dates, but I wasn't interested. I liked having our Upper West Side apartment to myself; it had seemed to grow overnight, morphing into a more masculine environment without her delicate female touches dotting everything.

There was about a month where I walked around in a fog, missing her, missing her company. I'd come home after a long day selling jewelry, something I'd somehow found I had a knack for in college and had parlayed into a lucrative position at Tiffany's, and settle into the silence. Friends invited me out for drinks or dinner, sometimes with their families, sometimes on our own, usually at bars crawling with people a good ten years younger than me. What was strange was that when women would catch my eye, or a friend would bring a single woman over, nothing happened. I'd smile and buy her a drink, listen to her lilting voice, but nothing was happening down there. I'd even walked one woman home and she'd leaned in to kiss me, smelling of peaches and vanilla, but I dodged her for a quick hug.

I figured that I just didn't have a high sex drive, that my friends and my softball team and my job and occasional noodling on the guitar were all I needed to keep me occupied. And the truth is, they were. Unlike my buddies who'd been devastated by their divorces, or the ones who had the opposite reactions, becoming consummate playboys, I was pretty much neutral. I missed Stella's presence, and her cooking, but that was about it. Our sex life had dwindled from its earlier passion to a half-hearted blow job from her here, a late-night quickie there, but we'd never really talked about it. I'd assumed sex was something you forgot about in a long-term marriage, and I truly hadn't missed it much.

I was surrounded by women most of the day, wealthy customers wanting jewels draped around their necks and wrists or hanging from their ears. Often they flirted as they waved around tens of thousands of dollars' worth of diamonds, telling me what the gifts were for, slipping double entendres into their rich laughs as they twinkled before the mirror. I liked helping them look more beautiful, but I didn't want to fuck them.

And then about two months after Stella was gone, my libido came back to life. Except it was like one of those movies where bodies get swapped, because all of a sudden, it wasn't women who were reviving my dick from its long dormant stage. In some ways, I was a teenager again: I started having wet dreams. I'd be asleep and I'd wake up remembering someone sucking my cock. The face and body would be anonymous, fuzzy, but the lips, and occasional stubble, and my own intuition, told me that these lips were not female. A man was sucking me off in those dreams, a man with a cock as hard as mine that he was either stroking or waiting for me to stroke. These unconscious blow jobs were always the best head I'd ever received. The dreams only came to me occasionally, and I'd wake up either having jerked off in my sleep, or needing to when I awoke, but they were so realistic, I felt almost like I'd gotten laid.

The dreams were starting to consume me, making me take after-work catnaps, hoping they'd return. I decided to see what would happen if I chose a more conscious route to accessing this brave new fantasy world. I picked a guy I worked with, one who I knew was gay, even though he never talked about it. You'd have to pick up some very subtle clues to know, but I've always had excellent gaydar—except about myself, I soon came to realize. He wasn't what I'd have guessed would be my type, but who knew anymore? He had shaggy dyed black hair that fell into his eyes, extra-pale skin, overly full lips, and thick black hipster glasses. He wore funky skinny ties and spoke softly, so you often had to lean in to hear him.

I spoke his name out loud: "Kevin." I felt myself open up, felt the fantasy step up a notch into something that could actually be possible. "Kevin, I want you to..." I paused because I honestly wasn't sure what I wanted him to do. But I knew if he'd been in the room, I'd probably be tongue-tied. I pressed on, though, determined to see what might happen when there was more than a nameless face in my big gay dream. I had never thought about what Kevin was into sexually. I tried to dredge up a story from our chats, but he was too circumspect for that. I decided, maybe because he was tall and skinny and probably weighed less than me, that he might like to be held down, maybe have his wrists tied together. Then his dick would be mine. I pictured it tall and skinny, like him, just perfect for my first time.

Sucking someone else's cock was totally different, even in my head, than getting my dick sucked. It was better, in a way, because I was in control; with my fantasy man's lips around my hardness, I couldn't control when I'd come, could only wait in perfect agony for him to work his magic. I shut my eyes and pushed two fingers into my mouth, trying to suck them in a sexy way, rather than just gulp. I whimpered, tears coming to my eyes. This was nothing like going down on Stella. Sucking Kevin's imaginary cock made goose bumps form all over my skin. My nipples hardened, my senses coming alive. I started moving my fingers slightly back and forth; even if Kevin were tied up, he could still raise his dick if he wanted. It was over pretty soon, because while I may have been in control of my mouth, my cock had other plans, and soon spurted a giant load of come.

I knew it wouldn't be long before I sucked my first real cock.

Seeing Kevin at work was a little awkward over the next few days. How do you come out as...newly horny for guys, probably gay, when you've been known for years as the married, straight, rather boring colleague? I couldn't pin on a rainbow flag at work, and in every other way, I was still me. It wasn't like people could tell just by looking, and I had a feeling if I confessed my fantasy to Kevin, he'd shoot me a look of great horror and scamper away. We weren't destined to become lovers, and I wouldn't have wanted to mix business and pleasure, anyway. Still, I observed him on the sly, wanting to be more like him, so at ease with his carefully coiffed hair and bee-stung lips, not caring who knew he was into boys, not girls. I felt in limbo, with my new desires loud and clear, while the rest of my life stayed stuck in the past.

One day, coming home on the train, reality caught up with my fantasies. My dick stood to attention when a sweaty young man rushed between the subway doors, fresh from a round of basketball. His brown curls clung to his head, his muscular calves topped by thighs that made me ache. I lifted my gaze and tried to read a subway ad for chewing gum, but my eyes kept darting over to him.

A seat opened up behind me and I sat, almost stunned at the visions swirling through my head. I reached for a copy of *Time Out New York* and placed it over my lap to try to hide my erection. When I looked up at the basketball player again, his eyes locked on mine, and he casually made his way over to stand right in my line of vision. His crotch was right before me, the outline of his cock visible when I took a quick peek. I flipped a page in the magazine, and he shifted so his leg was brushing mine. I probably looked a little bit crazy, a middle-aged man in a black designer suit, smooth shaven, surely blushing as I sat there with an aching dick hidden by a magazine as a young man, probably a college student, made me hard by brushing his knee against mine. Finally, my stop arrived and I stood, inevitably brushing against him. In a flash, he took my hand and let it trail over his cock. The whole thing took maybe two seconds, and I'd say I imagined it but I know I didn't because my dick shifted in my pants, responding instantly. You'd have to have been staring intensely to think it anything other than two passengers shifting to make room for one of them to exit, but my face burned with the truth as I rushed home.

I stood before the full-length mirror in my closet and jerked off, holding my cock and wishing it were the sweaty subway guy's, wishing I could've taken him in my hand, wrapped my fingers around his firmness for more than a single moment. I reached behind me and started to gently stroke my anus, which heretofore had been a sexual no-strike zone. I had so little experience with anyone's back door, but my finger there felt good. I pressed harder, knowing I'd need lube to get the job done right, but being too caught up in the sensations to pause for even a moment. I kept stroking myself, moving my fist up and down, thinking of the sweaty basketball player's face back there, licking me, opening me up with his tongue. "Yes, harder," I cried out and then opened my eyes and watched my dick shoot a veritable waterfall of jizz.

Then I met Felix. I can't honestly say I was looking for him; we were both on line at a Starbucks on the Upper West Side at eight in the morning on a Saturday, surrounded by strollers and families in what could have been Middle America. I was behind him, thinking about what I should do with myself that day. I still wasn't used to planning entire weekends. Then he turned around, just for a second, and I gasped. I just knew, the same way I had just known, in my earlier life, with Stella: God was speaking to me, telling me He had hand-delivered this fine specimen for my pleasure. And for all I knew, maybe he had. Felix turned and gave me a killer smile, perfect white teeth gleaming from a tan face with sexy stubble I suddenly wanted to rub my face against. "Hey there," he said in a sensual Southern drawl, and I returned his smile. There were a few people ahead of us so we had some time for chitchat. He was friendlier than most folks you meet randomly in New York, perhaps because, as I soon learned, he'd just moved here from Atlanta three weeks earlier.

He was a fresh-faced twenty-five, but that didn't stop him

from flirting with me, standing closer than necessary, and giving me this smile that, while blindingly white and seemingly wholesome, felt like it was speaking straight to my dick. Whereas I felt like a tongue-tied teenager at first, Felix was all confidence.

We walked outside and found a bench to sip our respective coffee and tea. I teased him about his English Breakfast with milk and sugar ("Do real men drink tea?") while he teased my decidedly nonmacho option of a caramel macchiato. I found out that he was looking for work, doing anything; he had two months until law school started and wanted to have fun and make some cash, but nothing too high pressured. I told him the briefest of details about my job, and finally, after a pause, he asked the big question: "So, are you single?"

He wasn't asking if I was gay, and I realized that by my having coffee with him, it was simply understood. I liked that; just by being me and talking to a stranger, I could be taken for gay. It gave passing a new meaning. "Yes, at the moment. I was with someone for a long time." I wasn't ready yet to give him the whole story. I did, however, give him my card, and he leaned over my shoulder, resting his chin on it as he dictated his number. "Nice to meet you, Mr. Perry," he said, all mock formality as he extended his hand. I gripped it and had the overwhelming urge to hug him, to smell his hair and hold him close. It was a different impulse than my cocksucking fantasy.

He emailed me the next day, a casual, *Want-to-have-lunch?* missive.

*Let's make it dinner. Tomorrow night. I'll cook.* The words were on my screen and then whizzing their way to his before I could rethink them—or overthink them. This wasn't the time to beat around the bush, not when my future depended on it. I needed to know whether I was really gay, whether this was just a rebound fantasy or something real.

I found out very soon. Felix replied and wrote, *You're on. I hope you can handle me. F.*

I wasn't sure what he meant and didn't want to ask. I took the next day off because I knew I'd be a wreck at work thinking about trying to get my place ready and planning a meal. I made chicken with eggplant and garlic, my specialty. For a minute, I considered leaving out the garlic, but I like the taste of it, and hoped I'd be tasting it on Felix very soon. He arrived promptly, bearing a bottle of champagne. His tan looked even deeper, but his smile was just as easy and relaxed. I went to hug him hello, then just put out my hand for him to shake.

Even that simple touch made me tremble in a way I wasn't sure I ever had before. This was now far beyond simple arousal; it wasn't just my cock that wanted to get close to Felix. "Would you like something to drink? Or a snack?" I asked, pointing to the plate of Brie and crackers I'd set out.

"A snack? Like this?" he asked, then leaned down and kissed my neck. Being shorter than Felix, even by just a few inches, along with the whole gay virgin thing, made me feel like I was the younger man. His lips on my neck sent vibrations through my body, and I had to lean on the counter for support.

"Felix..." Just saying his name, one so different from the one I'd gotten used to saying, felt rougher, more forceful than "Stella." Just like him. Felix turned me around and kissed me right on the lips. His tongue probed my mouth and I opened up for him, letting him take me.

I was hard, and no longer cared about our meal. "Take me to your bedroom," he said. I did, holding his hand all the way. I was glad we were skipping the preliminaries, because the last thing I wanted to do was dwell on the fact that this was my first time. That would be my little secret.

"Steven," Felix said throatily. "Take off your clothes. I'm

going to help you relax." I did as he ordered, sensing him watching me. When I was undressed, he told me to get on my hands and knees on the bed. "Head down, ass up." My cock was so hard, my mind racing, my body buzzing, I'd have done anything for him. The difference between being an adult and a fumbling teenager was that I wasn't about to come before things got interesting.

That's when I felt it—a smack on my ass. I'd heard of S&M, but my sex life with Stella had been strictly by the books, and I don't mean *Story of O*. I'd never thought much about it one way or another, and there was no time for thinking now. Felix kept smacking my ass, the right side, then the left, once again so sure of himself. I grunted in response, the pain a mere flicker before heat took over; heat that warmed not just my ass, but my entire lower half. "You're getting more comfortable, aren't you?" he asked.

"Yes. Yes, sir, I am." I had no idea where that came from, but there it was. Felix kept going until my backside burned, my fingers curled around the sheets, my teeth clenched. I wasn't sure whether to be relieved or excited that he had stopped.

"Now kiss me again." Taking orders from Felix was easy, even though I'd never done that before, either. Letting someone else run the show and tell me what to do, wondering what would happen if I disobeyed, all lent my otherwise drab bedroom an air of naughtiness. I'd say it was like an out-of-body experience, but I was there, 100 percent. I was there as Felix kissed me, there as he pushed my wrists down onto the bed, there as he hovered over me, pinching my nipples. I was there when he ordered me to keep my hands above my head, then brought his cock to my lips. "Take it, take it all," he demanded.

It was like in my dream, but a million times better. I wanted all of Felix—not just his cock, but his being—and the way to get it was to take him inch by inch down my throat. The smell drew me closer, then feeling just how hard he was. I opened my eyes to see the last inches of his hardness disappear between my lips. Then Felix reached his hand back to manipulate my dick.

"No," I halfheartedly protested, not meaning it. Of course it felt good—hell, it felt incredible—but I wanted to focus on sucking him.

"Learn to multitask," was all he said, and I couldn't really talk with a mouthful of dick.

So I did, enjoying his slowly pumping hand and his faster-pumping cock. I shut my eyes, knowing that there would be no going back. Felix's cock was speaking to me, and it was saying: *Welcome home*. He only lasted a few more thrusts before he was coming, right in my mouth, on my tongue. I'd been expecting it, but it was still a surprise. I'd stopped comparing everything he did to Stella—we were in our own world now—but tasting another man's spunk was a revelation. I'd tasted my own, but no one can ever be a good judge of that. I gave Felix's five stars for fine dining.

"Your turn," he said, and I watched as he jerked me off. We both looked on as I ejaculated far enough to hit the wall on the other side of the room.

I tried to downplay my response to what we'd just done. I didn't want to look foolish in front of Felix, or worse, to seem like the inexperienced straight guy looking just to get off. But our conversation over the delayed dinner was easy and comfortable, and I knew by the end of the evening we'd be getting together again soon.

It wasn't until a year later, on our anniversary, that I fully fessed up to my straight past. Felix wasn't mad, just curious, and we spent the rest of that night talking. The others we've spent otherwise engaged. You can only imagine (at least, I hope you can). I haven't exactly racked up huge numbers on my bedpost (though Felix promises to take me to a sex party soon), but I've learned that quality is quantity when it comes to sexual partners, and that when enjoying the finer things in life (i.e., cock), you're better late than never.

# THE BOY IN THE MIDDLE

Thom Wolf

The boy was waiting by the east gate of the university, just as we had planned. He stood at the bus stop, slouched against a post, smoking a miniature cigar. He wore a dirty pair of jeans and a navy hooded sweater.

His profile had said he was eighteen but he looked a year or two younger. I considered driving on without stopping but as he *was* waiting outside an adult college I let the age thing go. He looked up as I pulled over, threw his smoke into the gutter and got in the car.

"Hi," he said.

I looked him over carefully. His hair was dark and cut military short. He had deep-set eyes and a small stud pierced his bottom lip. His mouth was slightly uneven and sullen. Kind of cute, I thought, despite the attitude.

"Do you still want this?" I asked.

"Sure I do. I'm here aren't I?"

* * *

Jack was waiting in the living room when I brought the boy home. He was shirtless, a can of beer resting on his hairy belly. His eyes ignited on sight of the youth and he stroked his crotch as a mark of esteem.

The boy said his name was Jared. It seemed to suit. At fifty-five, Jack and I had been together for more years than Jared had been alive. If our age concerned him, it didn't show. From his first contact, an email containing a nude photo, Jared had actively courted us. The details in his emails were explicit, spelling out his need for older men. Much older men. *I want to get fucked*, he claimed; *fisted, double penetrated*. I thought his claims were over the top, just a tease, but the boy persisted until finally, six weeks later, he was here.

"Are you clean, boy?" Jack asked.

The boy answered like a soldier. "Yes, sir."

"Your asshole?"

"Absolutely. Ready for anything."

Satisfied, Jack popped the fly on his jeans, hauling out his big semihard dick. The boy got on his knees and swallowed. Jack put both hands on the back of his head and forced him down. Jared spluttered. I went to the kitchen for a beer. When I came back into the room, Jack was fully stiff and the boy's lips slipped up and down his pole at a constant rhythm. I lingered at the edge of the scene, watching. Jack told him to open his eyes and look at him while he sucked. The boy complied and emerged almost angelic with wide brown eyes, a furrowed brow, and his wet mouth stuffed with cock. Jack's hands remained on his head, guiding the pace.

I knelt behind the boy and slid my hands around him, unfastening his jeans. He wore cheap blue shorts that slipped from his ass with a whisper. He carried a little puppy fat around his rump. His skin was very white and his asscheeks were heavy, dusted with dark hair. His ass was ample in my hands. I opened him, looking into the hairy crack, at the rosy pink hole in the black. Breathing in the savory scent of his butt, I moved closer. His body shuddered when I began to rim him, swirling my tongue around the seam of his asshole, tasting fresh sweat. I slid a hand between his legs, feeling hairy, low-hanging nuts and a small cock that was still soft. I reveled in the youth of his body. It seemed unformed, underdeveloped compared with the flesh I was used to holding.

The lube was in a drawer beside the TV. I slicked up my fingers and started on his ass, sliding one into his warm tract, then quickly working three digits past his ring. Greasing his hot ass, I looked along the line of his spine toward Jack, whose eyes were half lidded as the boy slobbered on his dick. Despite my efforts I couldn't get a fourth finger into his tight snatch, his ring refusing to yield any further, but I was tired of finger-fucking, I was ready for the real thing.

I threw my T-shirt into the room behind me and shucked my jeans over my ass. I fisted another handful of lube over my cock and maneuvred the head into the crack, nudging his sloppy hole. He took the head easily, but his body tensed when I slipped deeper inside. Jack tightened his hold on Jared's head, forcing the boy's face into his lap.

"Take it, you slut. This is what you wanted."

Dick fully inserted, my hips pressed against his fat ass. I held him by the waist, routing him to my cock. We fucked the boy from both ends, stuffing his ass and mouth. I watched as tiny beads of sweat began to form on the smooth white curve of his spine. His ability to take it so passively, without complaint, urged me to go further, harder, faster, rougher. Soon, rivulets of sweat trailed down my own back, prompted by the rapid motion of my hips. His big asscheeks wobbled under the onslaught of my pelvis.

Jack released his grip on the boy's head. "Change places with me," he said. "I want to fuck that."

My stiff cock slipped out of his ass with a slurp, pranging its lubey head against my belly. I sat on the sofa while Jack took a turn mounting the boy's ass. If Jared had any misgivings about sucking a dick that came fresh from his backside, he was not deterred by them. He grabbed my shaft and his mouth went straight down onto it. Jack must have loosened up his throat because the boy had no trouble swallowing me whole.

After several minutes we flipped again. Turning the boy over onto his back, I reentered his ass while Jack squatted over his face and fucked it. The boy took everything we gave without grievance. His body was slack and willing, though his cock didn't show the slightest stiffness. I came first, draining my balls into the soft, warm depths of his bowel. When I was finished, shuddering through the tail of my climax, Jack took my place. He rammed his dick into Jared's come-sloppy ass, churning it over until his own heavy load merged with mine.

Later, the three of us stood at the kitchen door, still in our underwear, smoking. It was a drizzly afternoon and the garden was littered with brown fallen leaves. I was feeling good about the encounter, relaxed in the aftermath of sex. Jack laughed at the boy's miniature cigars and offered him a fat Don Julian. The boy toked on the big cigar, blowing smoke into the garden. He also seemed relaxed, less guarded than before.

"How many older men have you had?" Jack asked him.

"Only one," the boy replied, "besides you two. I used to meet a guy from Durham. He was forty-two. I thought he'd be able to teach me stuff, but he didn't. Not really. He just wanted to cuddle and fuck all the time."

I laughed. "And you don't?"

"Sure I do, but I want more than that. I want a man who'll use me. I want to be his boy."

"What does that mean?"

"I just want sex. I don't want dinner and DVDs. I want to be fucked, roasted, as many cocks as I can get. You know, like we did today. You guys didn't want to get to know me. You just wanted to fuck me." He exhaled a great cloud of smoke. "That's cool, 'cause it's what I want too."

"You're a strange kid," I said.

"Don't analyze me, just fuck me. Do what you want. Fuck me, fist me, stuff massive dildos up my ass; whatever you want to do. I told you, that's what I want."

I stifled a smile. His talk was the stuff of porn and overly imaginative forum chat. I guess he had constructed a fantasy image for himself—as an uberbottom—and was desperately trying to live up to his creation. I imagined he had an XTube profile and a whole gallery of videos recorded on his webcam. I'd seen plenty of boys like him online, spreading their asscheeks and stuffing themselves with every imaginable instrument. It was hot and entirely ridiculous at the same time. Silly boy, and yet his naivete was somehow endearing.

One week later I picked him up from the same spot. He trotted to the car and greeted me with an enthusiastic smile. He appeared different, brighter, more assured. The weather had made an unseasonable turn for the better and, although it was November, he wore a baggy pair of shorts that hung halfway down his ass and a tight, sleeveless T-shirt.

"How's it going?" he chirped. "Got something exciting for me today?"

Jack and I had talked long and hard before inviting him back. Jared was a horny little piece, and as a couple of old farts we were flattered, but there was something about him that raised doubts. I had serious reservations about getting involved. Perhaps it was the artifice of his person, the carefully studied behavior. We didn't know him; I doubted we ever would, no matter how many times we fucked him. We were old men. It was pleasing to think a young boy wanted us so keenly, but I had a niggling suspicion that he was trouble, and at our age we didn't need that.

I took him straight to the bedroom, where Jack was waiting in a loose pair of pants tented by his dick. Jared undressed in a hurry, flinging his clothes into the corner of the room. He wore a black jockstrap and kept his white socks on. It was a look I'm sure he'd lifted from porn. He dived straight onto the bed, releasing Jack's dick and going down on it like cannibal. He took it right to the root, deep-throating on the first pass. Jack closed his eyes and surrendered to Jared's lips. I undressed slowly, watching, listening to the wet slobbering sounds from the bed. Jack looked like he was enjoying himself. Despite my reservations I was hard before I slipped my shorts to the floor.

I got on the bed and grabbed hold of Jared's short hair. I dragged his mouth off Jack's dick and shoved him down on my own. He gasped and snuffled but his lips were around the fat root in seconds. I let him have it hard, holding his head in place while I rammed my cock deep into his throat. The boy gagged and made startling animal noises but I refused to release my hold.

"This is what you wanted," I said, fucking his face with an angry passion, surprising myself.

When I finally relented the boy sat back on his haunches, gasping for breath. Saliva drooled from his small chin, dripping down his neck and heaving chest. Jack got into a kneeling position beside me. I could feel the tension in his body, the tightly coiled excitement. He grabbed the boy's head and gave him a session of similar treatment, holding his face, sinking his cock into the depths of his throat. After a while we began to alternate, moving his face forcibly between our dicks. He had just a moment to catch his breath before we took our turns reaming his sweet mouth. It all felt wrong but I was *so* turned on, more than I had been in years. It was exploitation, dirty, almost like rape. I had to remind myself that this was exactly what he'd asked for.

My reservations were insignificant beside my zeal for the boy. I left Jack to his mouth while I started work on his ass. The boy had been perfectly explicit in describing the things he wanted us to do to him. I intended to give him just what he wanted and in the process learn how much of him was genuine, and how much was artifice. I lubed his butthole, paying attention to its tightness and size. It wasn't long before I was able to slip three fingers effortlessly back and forth through his sphincter, like a bolt in a well-oiled lock. His pink opening flourished and unfurled around my hand. When he was hot and loose, I opened the drawer beneath the bed, where Jack and I kept the toys.

*No point starting small with a kid like this*, I told myself, selecting a medium-sized dildo with an enjoyably fat head. The boy gasped and raised his hips higher when I introduced the wide tip to his butt. The next toy to stuff him was a corpulent black dildo with an unfeasibly thick girth. The boy made a sound that could have been a cry, if it weren't muffled by the meat in his mouth. I had to put some weight behind the base of the toy and force it through the resistance of his ass. Just as I began to think that this one was beyond him, his sphincter gave way and the fattest part of the dildo went in. I followed through, pushing the entire length deep into him. I fucked him with the big one, churning his ass into a sloppy mess, and when I finally withdrew, his hole was squelchy and beautifully slack.

I mounted him then, slipping my cock into his welcoming bowel, and despite the slackness of his hole, it was not long before I ejaculated a huge, gooey load into his ass. My come trickled from his anus when I pulled out and ran in a slow trail across his balls.

Jared wanted to return the following weekend. We concocted an excuse and declined him. The following week we were out of town, visiting friends in the country. It was almost a month before we agreed to see him again. As before, we'd considered the implications of having him over. Did we really want to involve ourselves further? My reservations lingered but there was something in the tone of his emails, the explicit detail of his text messages, which aroused me and made me want him. That third afternoon was much like those that preceded it; we ravaged his lips, forcing both dicks into his mouth at once. We fingered, fucked, and dildoed his hole. Just as we had with his mouth, we pushed both our cocks into his asshole. The boy screamed at the double penetration as he straddled my hips. Jack shoved in from behind while I was already in him. The boy's face contorted with the effort, mouth wide open, eyes shut tight. His small body lay between us, tight against my chest. I kissed his twisted lips as we fucked.

Jack and I took Viagra that day. Once we had both come inside him, it took just a short while to rouse ourselves back to a state of excitement. Jared lay back across the bed and we fucked him long and slow from both ends, taking it in turn to pillage his mouth and anus. His butt smelled strongly of spunk as we churned. He farted afterward, spurting the white gunk onto our sheets. He spread his legs wide and we scooped the come back into his hole. Afterward we lifted him into the bath and pissed all over him. He turned his face into the amber streams, opening his mouth, bathing in the shower. The boy smiled and piss poured from the corners of his mouth.

Our afternoons with Jared became an odyssey as we explored the limits of his body. The boy was never anything more than passive. He rarely got hard as we delved into his ass, and he never ejaculated. We put everything imaginable up his ass: toys, snooker balls, food. We gave him enemas of beer and milk and applauded the spectacular fountains that erupted from his hole. Once, with several loads of come inside him, he squatted and dumped the hot white stuff into a bowl, before pouring the butt-fermented spunk down his throat. Nothing was too much for him. He had no limits. Each day when we were done with him, he asked when he could come back. "Not another week," he complained, "that's too long. Can't I come over tomorrow?" I refused to acquiesce to his demands and kept a minimum of seven days between our meetings.

If he had another man on the go during that time, he didn't mention it and we didn't ask. On reflection we knew very little about him. He went to college but where he came from was a mystery. He didn't talk about friends or interests. He didn't talk about anything except the things he wanted us to do to him.

After a couple of months I began to lose interest. Despite the wild experiments, sex with him became routine. His passivity was predictable, boring. If he displayed any passion, any physical response to the things we did, it might have been different. But he took it all without comment or reaction.

I began to spank him, with my hand at first until I bought a flat leather paddle to use on his smooth white flesh. I used it hard, beating his rump until it smarted. The boy made all the right noises, gasping, crying, though I noticed there were no tears in his eyes. His reaction, like every other, was artifice.

"Same time next week?" he asked. "You gonna pick me up at the usual place?"

We were in my car, just the two of us, as I delivered him to the bus stop. He had a hand on the door, ready to bound off.

"No," I said at last. "Next week won't do."

His pretty face fell. "The week after then?"

"I don't think so. I think it's time we took a break."

"What?" his bottom lips thrust forward. "Don't you want me?"

The answer was no, but I broke it to him gently. "Jack and I are a couple. For the sake of our own relationship, we can't keep doing this. I'm sorry, Jared. It's not your fault, but you have to respect what we have. I'm afraid it's over."

It wasn't over. His messages, via email and text, continued. He sent photos of himself and short films recorded on his webcam. I deleted each message without response. The only way he would get the message was to cease all contact. After a while the frequency of his messages began to dwindle. Jack and I returned to a monogamous kind of normality. We didn't feel the need to prove our manliness or desirability by having sex with much younger guys. I continued to feel uneasy about the affair. I wasn't proud but in time I began to forget. It was easy to pretend it never happened.

Until the doorbell rang one Saturday evening in March. Jack was making dinner while I worked on my laptop in the study. The bell rang insistently, quickly followed by a rapid hammering. I knew it was Jared before I answered.

He swayed on the doorstep when I answered.

"Hey man," he pushed straight through into the living room. "Where've you been? I've been waiting for you."

He smelled of beer. But there was more to his behavior than alcohol. He was completely out of it. His pupils were black holes, his expression crazed and distant. He shucked his jacket off onto a chair and began to hitch his T-shirt over his head. His body was noticeably thinner than before. He'd lost muscle tone and his rib cage was painfully visible. I noticed a profusion of white stains on his pants.

"What are you doing?" I asked. Jack came through from the kitchen, his face stony.

The boy laughed, a sharp, hysterical sound. "I'm here to get laid," he drawled, unbuckling his belt. "Come on guys, do me! Do me right fucking now! Fuck my ass."

"I don't think so," I picked up the clothes he had discarded and threw them back at him.

"Come on. You want me. You always want me. My ass is good, good and nasty. I got a butt load of come in there. Nice and sloppy for you."

I stared at him, appalled, as he shucked his jeans down his skinny legs. His cock was a worm in an unruly nest of pubes, white and wasted. He came over to me, grabbed my hand and forced it onto his dick. It was cold and lifeless. I recoiled.

"What are you on, you idiot?"

He giggled and turned to Jack. "You wanna fuck me, don't you Daddy?"

"No. Get out." Jack's tone was uncompromising. It seemed to get through to the boy's addled mind. Jared's face slackened. He wavered in the middle of room. I thought for a moment that he was going to puke.

I offered to drive him home.

"Home," he repeated, and the word seemed to have no meaning on his lips. "Fuck you, you pair of cunts." He pulled his pants up, struggling with the fastenings. "If you don't wanna fuck me there are plenty of guys who do. Hundreds of guys." He retrieved his T-shirt and jacket and cursed us as he dressed.

I stepped aside as he staggered to the door. I looked at Jack. "We can't let him go out, not like that."

Jack shrugged. Jared had already gone. "He got himself into that state; he can get himself out of it."

Outside there was no sign of the boy. I searched the street in both directions but he had vanished. As I returned to the house and locked the door, I hoped, a little guiltily, that he was gone for good.

# FRAZZLED

Trebor Healey

Stan liked sunbathing nude at the gay beach on Sauvie Island, where he could usually get some action and also enjoy a day of reading and sun with his significant other, a schnauzer named Frazzles.

He'd been in Portland for five years, having escaped a decade of debauchery, alcoholism, and misery in Dallas, his birthplace and the home of his ex-wife, who'd divorced him two years into the spiraling debauch when he'd given her a case of crabs picked up from a Mexican truck driver.

He hadn't made the same mistake with men that he had with women. He kept it all very impersonal. Besides, he had Frazzles, who'd been with him through his Portland years. Frazzles had learned to spot Stan's type, and barked vociferously if Stan happened to be dozing off or looking in the wrong direction when one entered his cruising space.

Thus the generic blond stud now approaching was a given to receive Frazzles's summons—which got the man's attention, but also scared him off, and he veered hastily into nearby bushes.

"If a man's afraid of my Frazzles, he doesn't deserve me. I want no truck with a nelly queen who's afraid of a wee little schnauzer," Stan commented a little too loudly at the scurrying blond. "I bet you'd like to sniff his ass, though, eh, Frazzles?"

And the little dog barked affirmatively as Stan chuckled.

And then someone else would walk by, and the excited little canine would be in a tizzy, running in circles and barking exuberantly, with Stan guffawing and carrying on: "You like big cocks, don't you, Frazzles—you little size queen!"

Two sailboats cruised by, slowing down, and sporting a rainbow of bandanas in their rigging. Being color-blind, Frazzles was at a loss on this score, but he was no slouch when it came to detecting virility; he spotted someone for Stan on the second boat and ran toward the shoreline.

"Frazzles, I'm too fat to swim out after them, and I'm too old to draw them in, so stop your yacking," he shouted after his companion. But Frazzles was already heading back around, tail wagging, satisfied with having proven his worth. He was never persistent about consummation, which was difficult for his attention span anyway.

Two punkish boys arrived not long afterward, and Frazzles, spotting them, began to growl almost imperceptibly, sizing them up. Both were dark-haired and thin. They were also heavily tattooed, unshaven, and visibly stoned. Frazzles had been around Stan long enough to know that youth could sometimes trump all other characteristics in the cruising game, but he needed a little help on this one. Stan came to his rescue with a *shhhh*. Barking at drug-addled clubkids who probably hadn't had much sleep was decidedly not attractive, and Stan was quick to reach into his handy Ziploc and proffer a large Milkbone biscuit to distract Frazzles.

The two boys took off their clothes, laid down a sheet, and soon reclined, flat on their backs and staring vacantly into the empty blue sky. But not for long. Petting Frazzles's head, Stan felt it rise under his hand as the dog perked up when the boys began to grope one another slowly.

Then things moved quickly. The boys got up on their knees, hands at each other's waists, two Tom-of-Finland cocks bouncing around like a couple of jib booms in a strong wind, while Stan force-fed Frazzles another Milkbone, and with his other hand, began to fondle himself, enthralled with the scene unfolding before him.

He whispered in Frazzles's floppy ear: "What a treat, eh, Frazzles? I hope they fuck each other right here in front of us." Frazzles licked his chops, looking quickly back and forth between his master and the two studs—who did not disappoint.

They fell into a sixty-nine, all writhing green tattoos and moans of pleasure that intermingled with occasional pops as one or both of their sizable organs slipped out of a lustful mouth. Stan had a furious boner by then, and being that his attention was increasingly centered on it, Frazzles—overwhelmed by the action-adventure of it all—commenced to lick his master's balls.

Stan pushed him away. The last thing he needed was Frazzles in some Pavlovian spiral, focusing on his master's anatomy instead of on the anatomies of his prey. "You're man's best friend, not his fuckbuddy, you little slut!" Stan scolded him.

But his remonstrations fell on deaf ears, for Frazzles saw first what Stan had been dreaming of. One punk was up on one knee while the other rolled onto his back, and a condom was clumsily and quickly unwrapped by all four of their hands. When the one entered the other, Stan was beside himself, lost in a vision of throbbing veined meat, black pubic hair, and straining arm and chest muscles, which soon sent his semen flying like Ariel out of his stubby little cock, concurrently causing his schnauzer to bark maniacally, concerned ostensibly that Stan's "little death" was in fact the big one.

The boys—who were cumming as well—heard, and upon emptying their prodigious tools, commenced laughing out loud at the prone Stan and the hysterical schnauzer jumping about and sniffing his balls. Which only got Frazzles all the more frazzled. He was momentarily off and running in a beeline for the punks, who suddenly considered they may have offended the aggravated canine with their mirth. He circled them once, barking in a fury, then circled them again. Stan was sitting up and shouting at him, but Frazzles couldn't be dissuaded, and when he circled for the fifth and sixth times, the boys did what anyone would do—they threw something at him. The used condom, in fact. And Frazzles, elated, returned to his master with the prize, which Stan held up now like a severed head, calling out wildly as the boys laughed: "The fuck, the fuck; I've got the fuck."

# UNDER THE RUSHES

David Holly

*After talking it over with the people involved, especially Will Branch, I've decided to give a complete account of the events that occurred back in April of 2005. I'm only doing this because the news media got it all wrong. The national news turned Will and me into heroes and temporary media sensations, but we didn't deserve much credit. Here's what really happened....*

It was the first day of spring break week at Lithia College, so Will Branch and I pedaled our bicycles out to Foggy Fenland, which most people thought was nothing but a marsh, but where we had found a nice spot with a sandy shore where the refulgent sun hit full on. The mire was only four feet deep at its deepest, so it wasn't much good for swimming; however, the spot Will and I had discovered couldn't be beat for sunbathing and other activities that might require a bit of privacy.

Wearing only cutoff jeans with our T-shirts flapping behind us, Will and I bicycled over the elevated gravel road across the sun-drenched bottomland. Our path took us along the edge of the slough where waterfowl of brilliant plumage made their home. Two long-billed curlews were feeding along the rushes, and a great blue heron and several black-necked stilts were wading near the shore. Will and I braked as a family of brown rabbits hopped across our path. One little bunny sat up and regarded our bicycles with amazement.

"Jim Finch, do you smell the wild dill blowing?" Will shouted, breathing deeply. "That scent makes me want to pound your dick until you come like a milkweed."

We dismounted and walked our bikes through the rushes and tall cattail stalks with tops just budding until we reached our spot, a sandy beach basking in the sun and hidden from prying eyes by the tall rushes, scented herbs, and thick ferns.

Will untied the blanket from the rack on his bicycle and spread it on the sand. The picnic basket had ridden behind my seat. I lifted it off and set it on the corner of the blanket. Will was still standing, though he had kicked off his sneakers. He handed me a *dare you* look, so I unfastened my shorts and hooked my thumbs into the waistband. I slowly wiggled out of my pants until I stood glorious in my hot-pink thong swimsuit. Will's eyes regarded my well-filled pouch with approval.

"Your turn," I said and waited until Will had dropped his shorts, catching them with his toe and draping them over a clump of green reeds. In his golden thong, Will resembled a god of ancient Greek mythology. When I touched his thick cock through the cloth, my swelling dick pulled the back of my thong tighter into the cleft between my perky cheeks. I wiggled my proud ass and felt sexy as hell.

"I can't wait," I urged. "It's been a whole fucking week, Will. Let's do it before we eat."

"Do what, Jim Finch?" Will asked, playing innocent.

I stepped closer until my cock nudged his. "Let's do it now, Will. Right now." I twisted so our cocks rubbed hard. Will moaned, so I stripped his thong down to his knees. His cock bobbed, hardened to its full thickness.

My fingers found the head of his dick, just as they had years earlier in what was the first of a long history of giving each other pleasure. I fingered his dry cockhead with my fingers, stroking the top lightly with my thumb. Then I gripped his shaft with one hand and rubbed my palm over the tip.

"God, Jim, get the lube," Will moaned.

Laughing, I rummaged in our picnic basket. I pulled out sandwiches and bags of chips until I found the bottle that had slipped beneath the black raspberry beer. Will had decided to help me look, and his cock brushed my bare buns. A strange thrill shot through me, as though there was something I wanted—but I didn't know what it was.

We stretched out on our blanket and lubed each other. Will's hand was like an old friend on my cock: he knew how to jerk me off better than I knew myself. It was the same with me—time and experience had taught me the movements that gave him pleasure. When a guy pounds his own cock, he tends to give himself a break. He'll back off sometimes if the pleasure grows too intense. However, when you've got another guy beating your meat, he's not going to give you a break. Even when you beg for mercy, he's going to dig deep into your tingles and make you come harder than you can ever make yourself. At least, that was the way with Will and me.

My lubed-up hand was thumbing Will's dickhead in the way that drove him crazy, while he was stroking hard up my shaft and squeezing the head of my dick. Working at his dick and feeling my own getting ready to erupt into a series of orgasmic thrills, I looked past Will's pleasure-tortured face, his lips drawn back with the delicious agony that was growing within his dickhead, and saw the blue sky framed in the thick green rushes. Little finches, red crossbills, starlings, and a red-winged blackbird were sharing in our sport. The birds delayed their feeding while Will and I tumbled beneath them and prepared to spill our seed.

As the orgasmic ripples grew in my cockhead, a long-tailed weasel ran across our blanket, and the watching birds scolded him for his effrontery. It was if all nature stood in hushed expectation of our orgasmic tempest. We had attuned our bodies to the throbbing excitement of nature, and nature approved.

We moaned, we thrilled, we squirted our hot wet seed, we howled like beasts, wild, free of society's restraint, at one with the rushes, and the soft wind, and the chattering birds, and the waiting weasel. The orgasm was like thunder in my cock from the flashes of lightning in my brain. I knew I was shooting great streamers of semen, and I could feel the hot strands of wet spunk that spurted from Will's cock splattering upon my chest and stomach.

When the climax was past, we lay muttering softly, sounds that made no sense but were abundantly clear, as we rocked our hips lightly and fucked the last drops of semen out of our cocks, into each other's fist.

"Fuck, that was a good one, Jim."

"Yeah," I agreed, unable to come up with anything more intelligent.

"Want to do it again?"

"Of course. But let's eat lunch first."

Will nodded in agreement, for the long bike ride and the intense sex had made him hungry too. When we sat up, the little birds flew away with mistrustful conjecture, and the weasel faded into the rushes. I removed the caps from two black raspberry beers and handed Will his bottle. He looked at my hand, still streaked with his come, and took the beer from me.

I swigged from my beer before I removed the wrapping from my roast beef sandwich, thick with horseradish and sliced red onion, and took a hearty bite. Then I tore open a bag of cheese puffs and grabbed a handful.

A gaggle of Canadian geese saw me open the bag, even as Will opened the bag of potato chips. The geese were soon surrounding us, behaving for all the world like a group of old friends congregating to share in our riches.

"I doubt this is good for you," I told a goose as he beaked a cheese puff from my fingers.

"Probably worse for us," Will said, fending off two geese with a few chips while he stuffed a handful into his face. "If we keep eating like this, we'll be fatter than the geese."

I grabbed some of his chips. "Nah, we're young. We can eat whatever we want."

We were dressed in our thongs, having put them on before we ate. With the sun already warming our skin, neither Will nor I could forget the day the sun burned our cocks, and we couldn't beat each other off for two weeks. As I was sipping from my black raspberry beer, I noticed that the long-tailed weasel had returned to our blanket and invited one of his relatives along. I flipped them a couple of bread crusts, and within a few minutes, the bold creatures were eating chips from my hand.

"The birds are keeping clear of those guys," Will joked. "I'm surprised the ferocious little carnivores will eat bread and chips. Even the friggin' geese are backing off."

Close up, the weasels were lean and brown with pale yellow bellies. Including their black-tipped tails, they were about twenty inches long. Their eyes were strange, reflecting consciousness that stood between omniscience and nothingness.

Will had a more material impression. "The little buggers look like dicks," he suggested.

Abruptly the two weasels bolted and the birds beat their wings. "What scared them?" I asked, alarmed, but even as I spoke sinister shadows fell across us.

"Will you look at the fairy faggots, Brother Skeet," barked a harsh country voice.

"Looks like our informant was right, boys," came a horribly familiar accent. From occasional samplings of the radio's fulsome drivel, I recognized the tones of Brother Skeet, pastor of the Last Chance Church and founder of "God's Gonna Burn Everybody Who Don't Think Like Us."

I bounded to my feet and saw four pickup trucks parked along the gravel path. Neither Will nor I had heard them arrive, and I wondered how long these depraved, self-selected Christians had been watching us. What I did know was that Jack Skeet and his boys were the most intolerant, homophobic hypocrites walking and that they were extremely dangerous. There were rumors that they had tortured and lynched several men they suspected of homosexuality. It was a documented fact that following each murder Brother Skeet preached a sermon about "them hosexual prevorts what busted Hell wide open."

A redheaded dipshit named Frank Clink, whom I knew from my high school days, pointed at a tall chestnut tree across the path. "That un's got a good limb, Brother Skeet. We can string 'em up right yonder."

Skeet examined the chestnut branch with a critical eye. "It'll do fer a hangin' tree, Brother Clink. But before we send these two faggots to Hell, we're gonna have a little fun with 'em."

"You mean..." Clink spit out a wad of snuff and the other men giggled in anticipation.

"Yeah, just like we did with them other two. We'll fuck 'em

before we lynch 'em. Send the fruits to Hell with *C-U-M* in their asses."

Will had heard enough. Without warning, he kicked Brother Skeet in the nuts, and the preacher toppled with a shriek. Grabbing my hand, Will dragged me into the rushes. "Run, Jim," he urged, though I needed no urging. We ploughed headlong through the reeds, ferns, and cattails, running until our breath gave out, and then we fell to our knees and crawled through the muck. We had abandoned our clothes and our bicycles, so we possessed only the thongs that scarcely covered our dicks and left our asses exposed. Although, I suppose, we were trying to save our asses.

We crawled on our hands and knees for what seemed hours. I might have enjoyed the view of Will Branch in front of me, his bountiful ass cleft by his golden thong, were it not for the hunting cries of our dogged pursuers. Brother Skeet's oaths were the loudest: "Boys, we're gonna get them fuckin' fruits what kneed me in the balls, we're gonna buttfuck 'em 'till they faint, and then we're gonna string 'em up so the whole world can see the wages of sin is death."

"Amen, Brother Skeet," shouted his followers.

"Why do homophobes hate us so much?" Will whispered as we crept desperately through the rushes.

"Because they're queer but can't own up to it—even to themselves," I answered.

"Right on, Jim," Will agreed. "Look how their first thought was to fuck us in the ass. They're the *Queens of de Nile*."

"Do you ever think what it'd be like to have a dick sliding up your ass?" I whispered, watching his buttocks tighten as he crawled.

"I guess I'd give it a try sometime," Will said. "But not with Brother Skeet's mob."

"I didn't mean we'd put out for those assholes," I said. "I

was thinking about butt-banging each other. I'd take your cock anytime you wanted, Will."

For a while, we heard the men's pickup trucks racing down the cinder path and their calls to each other as they beat the reeds. We had been crawling through the mire for nearly two hours when I saw that we were approaching a clearing.

"Hey, Will," I said. "There's a cabin ahead with a big SUV parked outside. Maybe we can call for help."

Taking a quick look for our pursuers, Will and I sneaked to the cabin door. We had never traveled that far down the path, so we had no idea that anybody had built along the shores of Foggy Fenland. The cabin was a single-story dwelling, only about eight hundred square feet in size, though it appeared to be tightly constructed. Its poured concrete base lifted the beams above the marshy ground. The slough found its source in the Foggy Fenland directly behind the cabin.

"They must be duck hunters," I whispered to Will as we stood in considerable trepidation before the door. To knock or not to knock? Suppose the inhabitants were part of Brother Skeet's bunch? We'd be delivering our quivering asses to our hunters. Standing in only a pink thong as the sun dipped low in the sky above the rushes and a cool breeze rustled the tops of the ferns, I had never felt so chilled, so naked, nor so vulnerable.

Will looked at me, his eyes filled with questions. I drew a deep breath and rapped my knuckles upon the door. Never had a rap sounded so loud, and it was met promptly with a thunderous din as though a thousand dogs were woofing in warning. They sounded like gigantic dogs.

"Oh, crap," Will said as the door slowly swung open. He gripped my hand so hard that my fingers went numb.

"Mustard. Ketchup," came a ringing voice from inside. "Be quiet, boys. Do you want to scare the life out of our callers?"

Suddenly, standing before us was the most beautiful man I had ever seen—even including Will, though I wouldn't tell him so. Our host stood about five-ten, had frosty blond hair cut short, creamy skin, and perky muscles. I could see his muscles clearly because he was wearing only silk boxer shorts. His eyes traveled down our bodies, muddy, mucky, and scratched after our crawl through the bog, lingered over our thong swimsuits, and traveled back to our fearful faces.

"Hurry in, boys," he urged. "We don't want Mustard and Ketchup getting out and rolling in the mud."

Another man stood inside, holding the collars of two magnificent Golden Retrievers. Like his friend, he was good looking, and he was wearing only silk boxers. Once Will and I were inside with the door closed, the man released the two dogs. They promptly sniffed Will and me up and down and indicated that they would enjoy a good wrestle.

"Some men are hunting us," I blurted, stroking the dogs and fending them off at the same time. "They said they're going to rape and lynch us. Can we use your phone?"

"Rape and lynch?" the man who'd opened the door gasped. He glanced at his partner. "Boys, was it Jack Skeet and his bunch?"

"Yeah," Will said. Will and I introduced ourselves. The men told us that they were Hugh and Reggie. Reggie, the beautiful guy who had opened the door, told us to follow him.

"You boys need a shower," he suggested. "After that, we can find a way to get acquainted while we're waiting for Skeet's bunch to show up here."

"You're not gonna give us to them?"

"Hardly," Reggie said. "You boys are gonna have to trust Hugh and me."

Will and I stepped into the shower together, still wearing our thongs. After we'd rinsed off most of the muck, we pulled off our thongs and wrung them out. The warm water was a relief after our ordeal, and we began soaping each other. I was running a soapy washcloth up Will's buttcrack when the shower door slid open and Reggie joined us. My jaw dropped at the sight. Reggie looked even better naked. His dark, untrimmed cock was half-hard already, his gym-sculpted buttocks protruded enticingly, and his purplish nipples were swollen.

"Did Jack Skeet catch you boys jerking each other off?" Reggie asked to break the ice. "Oh, don't play innocent. Hugh and I have seen you in your hidden spot."

"I don't know," I said. "They arrived after we shot our loads, but they might've been spying."

"Yeah, they're sneaks," Reggie nodded. The shower door opened again and Hugh, naked as Reggie, stepped in. Hugh wasn't as strongly built as his partner, but he did have a sweet thick cock. His ass wasn't as muscular, but it was perky and rather girlish.

"Don't you guys do anything but beat each other's meat?" Hugh asked. "Don't you ever suck cock?"

Will turned red and his cock throbbed visibly. I grinned. Will and I had discussed cocksucking, but we had not yet worked up the nerve to try it.

"You haven't lived until you've felt a man's mouth on your dick," Hugh said. Hugh slowly slid to his knees before Will. As the warm shower spray beat upon his back, Hugh touched his tongue to Will's cock. Will moaned as Hugh kissed the tip of his dick.

"Don't you love watching them get hard?" Reggie whispered to me, directing my attention to his own swollen cock. Of course, mine was also soaring. And Hugh's.

Hugh licked down Will's shaft, flicked his tongue around his cock, and up the other side. He gave Will's cock a thorough tongue bath, returning repeatedly to the head where he kissed and licked the rim around the head and the very tip. Will's hands involuntarily clasped the back of Hugh's head, pulling the other man's face onto his throbbing erection.

"You ever thought about doing that?" Reggie asked.

"All the time," I confessed. I thought Reggie intended to suck my cock, but I suddenly realized that he was asking if I wanted to suck his. I was interested. I hesitated. "I've tried it with a banana," I acknowledged.

Reggie placed my soapy hand on his erection. "That's no banana, Jim. Keep gripping my shaft with your fist and go to work on the head with your mouth. You don't have to take it all. Just get a little taste."

Hanging tight to Reggie's cock, I slid to my knees. My hand drifted down his silky back until I was stroking his brawny butt. His cock stood solid right before my lips, and I slowly touched my tongue to its tip. The effect was electric—more of a lightning bolt. As my tongue tasted the tip of Reggie's cock, I distinctly heard a clap of thunder—the lights flickered.

One taste of his cock was sufficient. I was seduced. I was devoted to sucking it. I kissed the hood, mouthing it with my tongue and my lips. Without warning, without me thinking about it, Reggie's cock was traveling over my lips until I felt the base of his dickhead on the inside of my lips. Reggie hadn't moved, hadn't forced me, hadn't stuck it into my mouth. I had done it myself. I pulled back until it was out of my mouth, and as it brushed the outside of my lips again, I realized how much it belonged in my mouth. I wanted to suck it. I wanted to nurse on it, torment it with my lips, my tongue, my whole mouth, until it erupted and the creamy spunk coated my tongue and slid deliciously down my throat like a rich, sweet cream.

"That's it, Jim," Reggie moaned. "Suck me. Suck me off."

I rolled my eyes upward to see his face, which was unutterable bliss revealed, and over his shoulder I saw Will's face, near ecstasy from the ministrations of Hugh's mouth, yet watching me suck off Reggie with strange delight.

Even as I sucked Reggie, I knew that after this day my relationship with Will would be different. Before, we had made love as boys do, and although we would continue to masturbate each other, we would be open to new pleasures. I foresaw bliss such as I had never known.

However, that speculation only promised future bliss. Reggie's was the present cock in my mouth, and my hopes were wisps of smoke compared to the flesh I was going down on then.

"That's it, Jim," Will encouraged. "Blow him. Suck him off, Jim. Make him come in your mouth."

I sucked more furiously, gripping and stroking Reggie's fine ass with both hands while my mouth formed a hot chute for his dick. "Oh, Jim, you're doing it right," Reggie moaned.

"Ah, Hugh, you're gonna make me come," Will howled. "I'm getting real close."

I felt an electrical tingle and smelled burning sulfur in the shower. A close clap of thunder ripped the sky. Reggie pushed my head off his dick, and Hugh stopped sucking Will.

"Don't stop now," Will yelped.

"It's a thunderstorm," Hugh said. "Didn't you feel that lightning bolt? A direct hit might have killed us. We'll be safer on the bed. Besides it's time to switch."

Mustard and Ketchup were plastered against the bathroom door. When we pushed it open, the dogs leaped fearfully, woofing and yipping. Through the window, we could see wild lightning spears splitting the clouds and striking the ground in long terrible forks. The thunder became a din, and the cloudburst hit the cabin, the rain gushing down the windowpanes so heavily that we could see nothing.

The two dogs dived under the bed while the four of us piled onto it. "I guess that storm will send Brother Skeet and his mob packing," Will proclaimed as he stroked Hugh's cock. Those were Will's last words for a while. He discovered the delicious sensation of a cock in his mouth, and the only sounds coming from him were wet, sucking ones.

Events had pushed Brother Skeet from my mind, and I forgot him again as Reggie began licking my cock. As the storm snarled without, Reggie mouthed my cock and his hands stroked my ass. His fingers explored into my buttcrack while he sucked me, and the sensation of the intimate touch heightened my pleasure.

"Oh, Reggie, that's fucking terrific," I groaned. "Oh, yeah, you're sucking me so good."

Meanwhile, Hugh was encouraging Will, who was sucking as if he'd been born to the task. "That's the way, Will. Oh, fuck. Like that. Work the rim with your lips and tongue. Ah. That's the way. You're a natural cocksucker."

Inspired by the praise, Will rose to further heights, driving Hugh nearly mad with pleasure. I couldn't believe that Will and I had been such dunces. Yes, years of beating each other off had been great, but we could have been mixing masturbation up with some serious mouth action. "Just wait until next time, Will," I declared, my voice nearly a shriek as Reggie tongued my cock toward the edge. "We're gonna use more than our hands. *Even what we talked about earlier*."

The picture of Will and me sucking each other's cocks and of fucking each other in the ass was too much. I howled, "Oh, I'm getting close, Reggie. I'm gonna get my rocks off in your mouth."

Reggie stopped sucking immediately, and Hugh pulled his cock out of Will's mouth.

"Why'd you stop?" I yelped. I was in pain. I had been so close to the jumping-off place, the moment when I was going to orgasm no matter what, and Reggie had stopped with my dick teetering on the very edge.

"Nobody gets to come yet," Reggie proclaimed. "We're all gonna go off at once."

Hugh beamed. "We'll link up a four-way."

The rain was still coming down hard, though the thunder and lightning had ceased. The dogs remained under the bed as the four of us shaped a square. In the new arrangement, Hugh sucked my dick, I sucked Will's, and so on. That cock I had jacked to orgasm so many times was projecting toward my mouth. My eyes crossed in trying to look at it. I felt Hugh taking my cock into his hot mouth. Slowly I closed my lips around Will's dick and touched my tongue to the tip. He tasted of salt and musk.

Will made a low sound of pleasure in his throat. We were all so close to shooting our loads that I knew we would come right away. We'd gone to the edge of orgasm and stopped, and as we linked, we were a potential vortex of hard throbbing cocks, sucking mouths, contracting muscles, and rising semen. Will was leaking his seed onto my lips even as I took him into my mouth.

Hugh's mouth was a hot, wet, sucking chute. He sucked me hard and fast, until I found my own head matching his rhythm on Will's cock. Will was thrashing as he sucked off Reggie. Opening my eyes, I saw Reggie rocking in utter abandon, and I knew that he was coming in Will's mouth. Will had to be swallowing the ejaculated spurts; where else could they be going but down his throat and into his stomach?

That vision was with me as my cock tingled heavily. The tingles in my cockhead grew into an intensity that stopped just short of pain. The pleasure was rhythmic and enormous. Then my muscles contracted, shooting my spunk into Hugh's mouth. I tasted something sweet and salty, wet and slick, and I knew that Will was pumping his come onto my tongue. However, my own orgasm and ejaculations were so intense that I was hardly aware that I was swallowing Will's dick cream. I could only rock and thrust, nodding my head vigorously on Will's cock, abusing the head of his cock with my lips and tongue as I shot salvo after salvo of wet spunk down Hugh's throat.

The rain had stopped by the time we staggered into the kitchen. Will and I had dressed in our thongs again, while the other guys had slipped into their boxers. Reggie prepared gargantuan mugs of hot cocoa to which he added generous dollops of Bols *crème de cacao* and *crème de menthe*, and he set out a platter of colossal oatmeal cookies swollen with hazelnuts, black walnuts, and pecans, and dried apples, cherries, dates, raisins, and pineapple. "Hugh and I baked these earlier," he said. "Before we knew that anybody was *coming*."

We laughed at the pun, which seemed clever while we were all delirious from the incredible sex. We ate cookies and listened to the eaves dripping. Lured by the odors and our voices, Mustard and Ketchup ventured from under the bed. I slipped them a few bites though Reggie warned us not to gratify the beggars. I noticed that he broke his own rule.

While we were sipping from our mugs, Mustard and Ketchup bellowed a warning and rushed to the door. My heart leaped into my throat, and Will turned pale. Parting the curtains, I saw four pickup trucks stopping in front of the cabin. "Is there a back door?" I gasped. I had been having so much fun that I had completely forgotten about the indefatigable Brother Skeet and his flock.

"I've been expecting those boys," Reggie said.

"Persistent bastards," Hugh mused. "Probably hid out in

their vehicles during the rain and then charged up this way. We'd better get changed."

"What?" I gasped.

Reggie regarded Will and me with a steely gaze. "Remember when I asked you to trust us?"

"Yeah," I gulped, hardly able to believe that Reggie and Hugh would hand us over to Brother Skeet.

"This is it," Reggie said. "I need you boys to go out there and stall Skeet and his crew while Hugh and I get dressed."

Will and I exchanged a glance. After we had sucked cock together, we trusted Hugh and Reggie, so I pulled the door open, and Will and I stepped forth into the glare of the searchlights on the pickup trucks. Horns blew with malevolent glee as the preacher and his men fixed their lights upon our nearly naked bodies, our dignity preserved only by our minuscule swimwear.

"Who-ee, we got the tootin' fruits now, Brother Skeet," Frank Clink shouted, and his brethren echoed his malice.

"It's 'bout time. Get them thongs off 'em and bend 'em over the back of the truck," Brother Skeet shouted. "And see if there's more fairy boys inside that cabin. Boys, it's a good night for a bonfire."

"We're gonna burn 'em at the stake?"

"Damn straight. Give 'em a taste of Hell 'fore they get there. Help ol' Satan recognize his own."

We had to stall them for a few more seconds. I couldn't think of anything, but Will raised his arms, pointed at Brother Skeet, and intoned, *"I have said to corruption, Thou art my father: to the worm, Thou art my mother and my sister."*

Brother Skeet's flock stopped, gape mouthed, uncertain, looking to their leader for guidance. Jack Skeet looked like he was about to shit, and even I had never realized that Will could command such a dramatic presence, much less quote verbatim from the Book of Job. After a befuddled silence, Brother Skeet shook himself and screeched, "Lay hold of them faggots and search the cabin."

Rough hands seized Will and me, while two of the crew charged the cabin door. They had reckoned without the dogs, however. Mustard and Ketchup jumped against the luckless simpletons and knocked them backward down the porch steps. Behind the dogs came two men wearing state police uniforms. Reggie was holding his service pistol in one hand and a collection of handcuffs in the other. Hugh was brandishing a shotgun.

In less than a minute, Brother Skeet and his bunch were the ones bent over their pickup trucks while the two officers frisked and cuffed them. Will and I smiled beatifically as Reggie read the vigilantes their rights and placed them under arrest for attempted murder, attempted rape, attempted sodomy, possession of illegal weapons, possession of illegal substances, attempted kidnapping, assault, and assorted hate crimes. We laughed out loud when Reggie assured Brother Skeet that he would be spending the night in a secluded cell with the meanest, toughest butt fucker in the county jail.

A van from the jail arrived immediately, for it turned out that Hugh had alerted the sheriff before he ever climbed into the shower with us. Deputies had been watching the road, and when Brother Skeet and company moved in on the cabin, the law swooped down upon them.

After we watched the van carry Brother Skeet and his men off to jail, Hugh and Reggie drove Will and me back to our spot. Our bicycles were wet but undamaged, but our shorts, T-shirts, blanket, and picnic basket were soaked. Two reddish-brown muskrats were raiding the bags of soggy chips and the remains of our sandwiches. Still, the air had a clean smell. Wild geraniums had opened with rose and purple blossoms, and the rain had sprouted new growth on the quail plants, the winecup clarkia, and the naked bloomrape. Above our heads, a hunting owl hooted.

Will and I wrung out our cutoffs as best we could and slipped them over our thongs. Reggie patted my ass as it disappeared into the wet denim. "Guess you don't want to sneak into your dorm in a pink thong."

We loaded our bicycles and other stuff into our new chums' SUV. As we drove up the path, we saw a mule deer with grayish fur and new antlers watching us from the willows. Farther on, a bobcat, identifiable by his short tail, darted across our path.

"Glad we didn't disturb him while we were crawling through the rushes," Will quipped.

"Better a bobcat than Jack Skeet," Hugh commented.

Hugh and Reggie were reluctant to take credit for the arrest, and I wondered whether it was safe to be "out" if you were a part of the state police. The next morning, the media credited Will and me with capturing the gang. The *Lithia Ledger* headlined COLLEGE STUDENTS CAPTURE VIGILANTE KILLERS. Suddenly, we were heroes. That afternoon we received a call inviting us to a special celebration at the White House where the president would honor our bravery in a Rose Garden ceremony. We were scheduled for pick up by Air Force One for a ride to Washington with President Bush.

The next day, however, Will answered the phone, listened with an increasingly bothered expression, and announced, "It's all off. The White House. The Rose Garden. Air Force One. They refused to give a reason."

Grinning, I pointed to the campus newspaper's headline, printed just an hour earlier. The bold type read GAY STUDENTS TRAP CHRISTIAN HOMOPHOBE RAPE SQUAD. It was a truth the White House couldn't swallow.

The case didn't come to trial until August, after Brother Skeet's church had gone bankrupt paying for his defense. Will and I testified, as did Reggie and Hugh. Brother Skeet's lawyer cross-examined us vigorously to no effect. In the end, the jury found the whole bunch guilty, and Judge Cross sentenced each one to twenty-five-to-life. Judge Cross even assured Brother Skeet that he would gladly sentence him to lethal injection if evidence surfaced of his other rapes and murders.

Will and I became the two most famous students at Lithia College, but our new fame didn't make us forget our friends. Every weekend we bicycled along the slough to the Foggy Fenland. Sometimes we met Reggie and Hugh at our favorite spot, and other times we went directly to the cabin where Mustard, Ketchup, and their owners greeted us with joy.

# 8 BEAUTIFUL BOYS 8: THE FOLLIES REVISITED

Jamie Freeman

The room is dark when I first enter it.

It is familiar even though it has been fifteen years since I first came here, and perhaps a decade since my last visit. This place will never change. The Follies will live on, year after year, each season featuring a new crop of twinks treading the boards with reckless abandon. Each evening the more seasoned members of the company will drink vending machine coffee and read newspapers in the lobby between scenes.

I played here at the Follies most Saturdays while I was enrolled in an expensive university in Northwest D.C., learning to become a foreign service officer. I ducked my straight friends and became a regular at the matinees. The theater became a playground, or perhaps more accurately, a laboratory for my sexual awakening, providing me an unending stream of unattached bodies with which to define the stats for my personal ad.

It was here that I got the first blow job of my adult life, in one of the filthy theater seats only a few feet from where I am standing now. I lean with my back against the wall and look down at them, thinking that perhaps in this seat, or that one in the next row up, I once sat in my Levi's and black UCLA sweatshirt, trembling with fear as a man settled into the seat next to me. I remember the feel of his hand on my knee, then my thigh, then his fingers unzipping my pants. He was black with a handsome profile and a sweet smell, like stewed cinnamon or nutmeg. I remember his hands descending into my pants, my hips moving to allow him to pull them down and my dick out. I remember his hand coaxing me to erection and then, unexpectedly, expectedly, his soft, warm mouth descending on me, that feeling of softness and envelopment. His hand stroked me and his mouth caressed me with practiced skill. I was transported back to childhood experiments, backyard antics, then yanked forward into the sight of the writhing professionals fucking huge on the giant screen in front of me, into the depths of my crotch, into the deep throat of this kneeling man, into a world beyond childhood. And I came, and he sucked and sucked, as if he were afraid of losing even one drop. And it was over. I lay back exhausted. He thanked me quietly and left in search of another cock. I tucked myself back in, regained my strength and my composure, and eventually made my way to the exit, not realizing until I was on the Metro, staring distractedly at a beautiful blond boy in khakis and a white oxford, that I had a streak of dried, glistening come on the front of my sweatshirt.

Now, as I let my eyes adjust, the well-remembered smell of poppers and sweat and rot and sex assaults my senses. The room is warm today, almost humid. The spectators are a mix of older men dressed in business drag, postclones in the jeans and T-shirt combo, Capitol Hill wonks in immaculate white oxfords and khakis, and twinks in shorts and tight T-shirts.

As I stand here in the semidarkness, I feel a vague sense of physical connection to the shabby glory of the place. I look up at the peeling wallpaper and dark fittings and I know that, although I will forget the men, I will not forget the Follies. This place has a solidity in my memory that assures it of immortality. The feel of the Follies is one that I can summon at will, like a familiar physical sensation, the feel of my fingers curled around the knob of my childhood bedroom door or the feel of a favorite faded sweatshirt against my arm.

It has changed over the years, the old film projector removed, the back stairs and projection room converted into a warren of tiny cubicles and an upstairs room with barred windows. Men walk back and forth through the labyrinth, restless, caged, emerging on the far side of the room, walking down the far aisle and disappearing into a long hallway that runs, if it too has not changed, behind the screen.

I remember a man giving me a blow job back in that hallway of cubicles, and I try to recall anything about him. I have the sense that he was older than me, a little overweight, perhaps. I recall white cotton as if he were wearing a white oxford, though there is no clarity to the memory. This man who sucked me off so eagerly was just one in a long string of men on their knees, as anonymous as blades of grass in the lawn of the house where I lived at the time. And to him, I suspect that I too was merely one in an endless parade of boys dispensing their charms onto the soft expanse of his tongue, another pair of rounded buttocks to be groped, another choking sensation to erase the dull, dry residue of career, family, debt, and home-ownership. We shared a moment that afternoon, reading from the same script for a while, coming together for our separate purposes and, although I now have only the vaguest recollections of the scene, it seemed important at the time, a pivotal moment. There was something about it I thought I would remember always, but it is gone, washed away in a sea of other blow jobs, other bit players.

Today, nearly fifteen years later, I look around the room. There are so many older men, many long past the age of retirement. I make my way through a group of men who stand around the entrance to the passage at the back of the room, mock nonchalance cracking as I pass between them.

Their heads follow me: fresh meat.

I glance into the cubicles, climb steep wooden steps to the old projection room, and watch disinterestedly for a moment as a fat man gives a thin older man a blow job, the flickering movie barely visible through the barred window above the kneeling man's head.

I stumble down the stairs in the semidarkness and make my way across to the far side of the theater, nothing piquing my interest. When I emerge back into the theater and cross the back aisle in the direction of the door that I came in, there is a disturbance behind me.

I move aside and a cute blond man in matching yellow soccer shirt and shorts passes by me, grabbing the sleeve of my T-shirt and whispering "C'mon." I look at him in the flickering light from the screen and, seeing something attractive there, follow him across the lobby into a warren of connecting rooms, through another series of doorways, and into the restroom. Behind the restroom door is an empty shower stall, the knobs long removed, the pipes capped, an opaque shower door still intact, closing off the little cubicle from the world. He pulls me inside and kneels in front of me, hands already on my crotch by the time I have closed the door.

I am not hard, but within moments, blood rushes to my crotch as his hands and his mouth assault me.

"Wait," he says, jumping up and pulling his shorts down and

over his white sneakers, flinging them onto the filthy tile floor of the shower stall. "Do you like my diaper?" he asks grinning.

"Sure," I say, more curious than surprised.

"Yeah, baby, you're so hot. I just love hot guys to see me in my diaper. Yeah." He kneels back down, one hand rubbing his boner through the front of the diaper, one holding my cock against his frothing lips.

"Let me see your dick," I say, leaning back against the wall of the shower stall and looking down across my chest and stomach at his tight white diaper.

He pulls his dick out and strokes it a couple of times. It is small, thin but well-shaped, not too thick, but not tapered to nothing like many I have seen. He himself is short, lean, compact. He reminds me of my ex, Robert, but not as beautiful, not as sculpted. I remember Robert, muscular and nearly naked in his diaper at Halloween last year, and smile.

"You like it?" he asks. "You like my thick cock sticking out of my diaper?"

"Yeah, yeah, I do," I whisper, though in truth, the diaper does nothing but distract me and obstruct my view of his dick.

He returns to my dick, his throat opening to take it all in.

"I'm gonna shoot my load," he announces, too soon. "I'm gonna shoot my load all over my diaper."

I look down at him in silence, wondering where this all came from, how he became this particular person playing this particular role, in this particular place. Too many steps to contemplate, I suspect.

"You ready?" he asks.

"Uh, not yet," I say, somewhat surprised as I see him shudder.

"Yeah, baby," he moans. "Look at me coming in my diaper. Yeah, oh, yeah."

"You came?" I ask, trying not to sound incredulous, watching as his erection fades within the confines of the diaper.

"Yeah, I did. Sorry 'bout that." He leans back on his heels and reaches for his discarded shorts. "Maybe next time we can both come."

"Yeah," I agree, slipping my half-erect dick back in my shorts and watching, puzzled, as this little sprite of a man jumps up and flits out of the shower stall.

I follow diaper-boy into the lobby and duck back into the theater.

I wander in and out of doors, past old men in shirts and ties with cuff links and tie tacks; past an overwhelmingly ugly but jovial overweight man who laughs and says, "Hey, didya notice we're the only ones here under seventy?" in a tone that implies that we have enough in common to spark a rousing physical encounter. I smile and walk away.

I brush off a dozen wandering hands, rows of questioning eyes, a score of whispered promises and pleas. "I'd love to get that knob in my mouth." "Just let me have a piece of that and..." "If that thing gets hard, come find me, 'cause I'd love to suck on that for a while." "Hey, hey, you, come over here, come here."

A young man in a white shirt and dark tie with scared eyes wanders in, poses for a while, sneaks clandestine looks at me. I wonder if he sees in me a compatriot in this land of geriatric, overweight, homely, marginalized men, this world of darkness and age. He is a beacon to these men, many of whom doubtless see themselves in his visage. They see themselves as they were before the wrinkles and the liver spots and the sage of encroaching old age took them firmly in hand. His crisp white shirt and immaculate hair seem out of place here, ivory tower meets sewer tunnel.

We fail to connect although our eyes dance a slow, furtive

waltz. I reach out with my eyes above the chaos of his flustered appraisal of the room; he looks at me with immobilized hunger and bolts, disappearing out the front door, unfulfilled.

I wander out of the theater and make my way into a smaller room off the lobby where terraced seating faces a sextet of cubicles and a large television playing Hungarian porn. The step-like seating is covered with rough indoor-outdoor carpeting, for cleaning purposes, I suppose. I picture a bored man in flip-flops and shorts with a green garden hose spraying away the accumulated coded residue of a hundred million genetic dead ends.

Or perhaps the carpet is never cleaned, I think, noting the dark, ballooning stains and the thick smell of proteins, reminding me of chewed graham crackers. I also smell amyl nitrate, cigar smoke, sweat, shit, urine—all the primal smells that I have come to associate with the underground meeting places of my tribe, the smells below the dance floor, behind the curtains, in the bedrooms and bathrooms and basements of the world.

I climb up on the platform and watch the video for a moment. A black-cassocked priest is talking to a peasant boy while a knight stands listening outside the door. Their mouths move with unfamiliar cadences, and garrulous voices speaking heavily accented English have been dubbed onto the soundtrack.

A man walks into the room from the darkened hallway under the television, looks up at me, starts to walk past me, then stops, interested. I have seen him before, in the dark cubicles, in the theater, alone each time, interested eyes peering out from a Germanic face. He is short like the diaper boy, like Robert, and handsome, blond, in his forties, with a tight chest, flat stomach, strong legs. When I first spotted him, I thought his T-shirt said AMERICAN across the front, but upon closer inspection, I realize that it says BANANA REPUBLIC. He holds a Diet Coke can in his right hand, heavy gold link bracelet accentuating thick, muscular wrists and well-formed hands.

He looks up at me, then flicks his eyes in the direction of the cubicles.

I raise a speculative eyebrow.

He grins.

I remain stoic for some reason, nervously immobile.

He walks over to one of the cubicles, leaves the door standing conspicuously open.

I feel a response in my pants, my stomach, the back of my throat.

I follow him.

He smiles when he sees me, evoking a nervous grin from me.

I turn to lock the door; he turns to set down his drink.

He wraps his arms around me, running his fingers up inside my shirt, kissing the side of my neck, my earlobes. He pulls back a fraction and I expect him to kiss me, but instead he whispers, "Can I suck your dick?"

I nod and he drops to a crouch, his fingers nimbly reaching for my zipper.

He has my soft dick out in his hands, massaging it, licking the tip and nuzzling my balls.

I look to my right and realize that the cubicle wall is incomplete and a figure in the next cubicle stands watching us in the darkness. A small television monitor above my head splashes enough light into the cubicle to spotlight me and prevent me from seeing clearly into the darkness beyond.

The blond man between my legs has finally hit upon a rhythm, speed, and texture that sends goose pimples marching out across my thighs. I groan and lean back against the wall. He turns me so that he can sit on the low bench across from the television, his hands digging into my hips.

"Oh, yeah," I whisper, looking down into his pretty blue eyes, his lips pursed around my shaft. I smile and see the softening around his eyes that, were his mouth not full, would have relaxed across his face in the form of a smile.

He pulls back and I stroke myself, his saliva slick and warm against my skin.

"Are you gonna give me some of that hot come?" he asks, grinning.

"Pretty soon," I inform him, touching the side of his head ever so gently with my left hand.

Well-trained, he responds to the slightest touch of my hand and returns to the rhythm that threatens to engulf me.

"Yeah, oh, yeah," I breathe.

He speeds his efforts, fingers playing along the base of my dick.

"Oh, wait, wait, I'm gonna come," I say, touching his head with both hands, but he does not relent. Instead he redoubles his efforts and a wave of sensation hits me. I feel the first floodgate opening, a precursor, a clicking that resonates up from my balls. Then the flood reaches the tip of my dick and spurts into his mouth. He moans with what seems in my weakened state to be contentment, then holds my hands so that I cannot withdraw my dick and drains me dry, his tongue lapping and his cheeks sucking, drinking deeply.

I groan and sigh, then laugh as the sensations turn from the heat of explosion to the warmth of aftershocks that flow like waves and almost always seem to carry my laughter.

"Did you like that?" He comes up for air, finally.

"Yes," I sigh, still leaning back against the back wall of the cubicle.

He stands and begins to arrange himself.

"I haven't seen you here before," he says.

"I haven't been here in a long time," I reply.

"I'm Jack, by the way," he says, putting out a hand in what seems a disconcertingly formal gesture considering.

"Jamie," I reply, taking his hand, noting the manicured fingernails.

"Well, I hope I see you again, Jamie," he says, brushing past me to leave the cubicle.

"Yes, definitely," I say, smiling again.

He grins and disappears into the anteroom and I walk back into the theater, watching a knight deep-throat a peasant boy. I lean back against the carpeted step behind me and draw my knees up in front of me. I wrap my arms around my legs and rest my chin on my knees, gazing past the boys on the television and remembering my Follies.

# SMOKE AND SEMEN

Jeff Mann

Fireplace weather. That's what my partner Nathan calls this time of year, late October, when maple leaves turn the orange-red of a cigar's ember and pumpkins of the same color gleam from porches throughout our little neighborhood of German Village. The evening air grows chilly; gray rains fall; leaves pile up along the cobblestones; Nathan longs for a fire. Sometimes he uses quick-light logs from the grocery store, but more often he buys a load from pickup-truck men who sell wood on the outskirts of town. Most autumn and winter nights we spend in the living room, watching TV or reading, while logs pop and hiss on the hearth. Nathan likes to light candles around the room too, those cozy evenings. I've never told him why little points of fire haunt me, why the restless glow in the grate makes me sad. I don't want to spoil his pleasure. There's no need to speak of Aidan. There's no need to speak of something that happened so long ago.

* * *

Smoke and porn introduced us, Aidan O'Neill and me. Odd combo, I know. I was twenty-five, a grad student in theater at Virginia Tech, living out on Mount Tabor Road in a shitty but affordable trailer surrounded by woodland. One spring night around two A.M. I woke to the smell of smoke. I checked the coffeepot, the stove. No problem there. The odor was acrid, like burning plastic. I was scared, but I stayed calm, called 911, then sat out on the stoop till firemen drove up.

Aidan was the first one of four to stride into my smoke-hazy place. He and his compatriots located the electrical fire behind a wall and snuffed it, then advised me to call the landlord and demand complete rewiring and a smoke detector. By the time they'd driven off in their emergency vehicle, I was so disturbed by Aidan's dark good looks that I couldn't get back to sleep. Jacking off to thoughts of topping him, I wondered if I'd ever see him again.

Then and now, I'm small and lean, five foot seven, fit and smooth-chested, but, then and now, I'm into exactly the opposite kind of man—older guys with beards, body hair, and brawn. Daddy Bears, that's the phrase, and a Daddy Bear Aidan surely was. Even with his physique blurred by that bulky uniform, I could tell, admiring him that smoky night we met, he was everything a Bear chaser like me relishes: six feet tall, about forty-five, deep blue eyes, full black beard turning silver at the chin, bulky arms and torso, black chest hair thrusting assertive tufts over his uniform collar.

When, a few weeks later, I finally saw my Black Irish Bear naked, got to run my hands through that curly fur coating his chest, belly, and back, I was hooked. He loved Jim Beam, Bud Light, Sonic hot dogs, sausage biscuits, fruit pies, and doughnuts, so his hairy beer-gut vied with his thick pecs for most prominent physical feature. I loved his beefy chest, the curves of his belly, his incongruous little scholar's glasses, his redneck accent, even his oddly contradictory enthusiasms for Puccini, boxing, and ancient Greek and Roman literature. I loved the way the hair between his asscheeks would tickle my nose when I rimmed him, the way he'd gulp and choke when I fed him my piss in the shower, the way, during our sex games, once I had him bound, he'd pretend he was a kidnap victim and would shout for help into his gag as I shoved him across the bed, climbed on top of him, and ass-fucked him stupid. "Shut up," I'd snarl, slamming into him, clamping a hand over his mouth. "No one can hear you, bud. No one's gonna help you. Shut up and take it!" Beneath my grip, he'd toss his head from side to side, bucking like a rebellious mount, and shout louder. His struggles and my ruthlessness made us both very happy.

I loved all of Aidan, I guess. But I'm getting ahead of myself. This is how I skirt the sadness, by concentrating on the best parts.

We might never have crossed paths again if it hadn't been for those muscle-Bear DVDs. Startled by the smoke, I hadn't thought to hide them before the firemen came, and Aidan had noticed them on my coffee table. It took him a while to get up the nerve to come back. He told me later that most guys like me—young and slender—never gave him the time of day, but he figured, seeing those DVDs, that not only was I gay but I might be into men like him. So there he was, sitting in his Jeep in my driveway when I got home from class one drizzly April dusk two weeks after I called 911. He grinned at me through the rain-spotted windshield—big white smile set off by the bushy dark of his beard—rolled down his window, waved a Bud Light bottle at me, and asked if we could talk. Thick black hair fell over his blue eyes. Captivated, I invited him inside. Two hours later, dead soldiers littered my coffee table and we were naked, sixty-nining on my bed.

It took us a few months of vanilla sex to come around to what we really wanted. Who would ever imagine a thin young twink like me would be dominant, a big Daddy Bear like Aidan would be submissive? The butcher a man is, the bigger the bottom, that's what I'd heard here and there, and Aidan proved it true. Ever since I was a precocious pubescent, I had been fantasizing about making a warrior my slave—blame it on cartoons and comic books. I found that slave in Aidan.

Nathan's gone tonight, attending a conference in D.C. Rain's falling, hard and steady, over the quaint brick houses, slate roofs, and limestone stoops of German Village. Home from a hearty meal at Juergen's Restaurant, I shake off my umbrella, shrug off my jacket, and put *Tosca* on the stereo. Aidan loved Puccini's music because it was passionate, rapturous, and tragic. I light one of the quick-start logs, pour out some port, and, sipping, watch the flames. Aidan preferred to be pretty buzzed on bourbon and pot when I topped him; I guess chemicals helped him deal with the shame his craving for vulnerability and submission inspired; it helped blunt the sharp and hurtful edges of his double life. What I loved about him was his manliness, but that manliness, I came to know, was fractured with conflicts. How could a big strong fireman admit to being gay, much less a sexual submissive, the part-time slave of a boy half his size and twenty years younger? That's why he stayed closeted, I guess, why we never lived together, why our lives never truly meshed, despite his professed yearning to be owned completely.

Pyromancy, fire-gazing: that was one of the ways diviners used to peer into the future, seeing events to come in the quiver of flame or the shimmer of embers. It's not the future but the splintered past I want tonight. I gaze into the fire and try to see Aidan as he used to be.

The Cellar's just another smoky, noisy, college-town basement bar. Been working here since I started grad school, busing tables and bartending to make spending money. I'm pretty sick of it, but now Aidan shows up for happy hour when his firehouse schedule allows, and that adds a tasty edge. It's my break, so we sit side by side at the bar, late-afternoon sun slanting in through the wide plate-glass windows. I sip tonic water, he sucks on a double bourbon, we speak in undertones. If folks in this bar knew what we were talking about, they'd fall out of their chairs.

I study Aidan, relishing his rough looks: dirty jeans, muddy work boots, a camo cap with VIRGINIA TECH emblazoned on it, the black *300* T-shirt I bought him, extra large but still tight over his chest and belly. STAND, FIGHT, AND DIE, say the letters across his wide back. Not only is he a sucker for Greek and Roman lit, he's crazy about action movies where heroes swing sharp blades, and he's very proud of his sword and knife collection, his *Lord of the Rings* and *300* collectibles. So many things about him—his quirky enthusiasms, hot temper, insecurity, and need for praise—remind me of a little boy. Sometimes, despite the age difference, it feels like I'm the father, he's the son.

"You obeyed me?" I ask softly.

Aidan nods. He sips his Beam.

"Slave collar?"

"Yes, Sir." He thumbs aside the top of his T-shirt, and it glints darkly, the chain I ordered online. Beneath his shirt, it's secured around his neck with a padlock no one can see, a lock nestling in his chest hair, over his breastbone. The chain was silver when I gave it to him, when he fell to his knees before me and I first locked it around his neck, but since then his sweat has tarnished it. The links are black in places, as if stained with smoke. Silver and black, like his beard and body hair. A fine match.

I smile, satisfied. I enjoy giving him orders. He's happy to obey. "Balls?"

"Tied up, like you said. That thin, rough cord you told me to use. Kinda overtight." He pushes at the crotch of his jeans with the back of a hand and grimaces. "Hurting a little."

"Plug?"

Aidan grins. Why he's shifting on his bar stool is, I know, so he can feel the thick rubber up his ass. "Yeah, you bet! Been in there since my lunch break. Feels great. Been fun hanging around the firehouse knowing that...well, the guys would shit if they knew."

I clink my glass against his. "Here's to ridge-runner warriors and their scandalous secrets." I know Aidan loves it when I call him a warrior. Well, he is. Firemen are at risk every day. That's a fact I still have problems living with.

"Sir?" Aidan suddenly sounds shy. He pats his left shoulder. "Tattoo's almost done. Sean'll finish it tomorrow afternoon. I sure hope you like it."

"Good boy. I can't wait to see it. Tomorrow night, right? My place? I'll be home by seven. You still have tomorrow off?"

Aidan nods. "I'll be there by five. I have kind of a surprise in mind. I think you'll like it...."

The sun's set, the bar's grown dim. In that twilight, I nudge his knee with mine, finish my tonic, then head back to the kitchen to start my second shift.

Country dark, crazy November wind, tail end of a faraway hurricane, rubbing itself hornily against the hills, rippling the dead meadow-grass, shuddering the trees, robbing them of their last leaves. I'm a good hour late, taking the curves of Mount Tabor Road fast. Aidan's probably pretty pissed by now. Promptness means a lot to him. I tear my rusty old Civic up the driveway, park, bound up into porch-light glow, and hurriedly unlock the door.

Warm, dim and silent inside the trailer. In the kitchen, the stove-hood light's been left on low. Smell of beef stew, Aidan's Crock-Pot specialty, to celebrate our six months together. Bottle of red wine opened and left to breathe on the counter beside two glasses. One soup bowl on the kitchen table, another on the linoleum floor. Hanging my jacket on a hook, I shout, "Hey, I'm here! Sorry I'm late! We were slammed at work!" No Aidan curled up on the couch where I expected him to be, reading Virgil or watching a boxing match. "Hey, Aidan?" I call. "Where are you?" There's a flickering glow at the far end of the hallway, so I head in that direction, toward the bedroom.

"Well, well...damn. Damn, buddy, damn."

That's all I can mumble, leaning against the door frame, then standing by the side of the bed. For several minutes I just stand stunned, smiling at him, my cock stiffening in my pants. Here's the surprise he spoke of. What I'm feeling right now, I'm guessing, is bliss.

Aidan lies on his right side, long-lashed eyes blinking at me behind his round glasses. He's wearing nothing but his slave collar, the jockstrap I bought him, and a loose bandage on his left shoulder, taped over his fresh tattoo. He's roped his feet together and cuffed his hands behind his back. Beneath the bit-gag, his mouth is stuffed with the smelly, stained rag I've been jacking off into for the past month. He's never looked more beautiful, more manly, more powerful.

Around the room, votive candles gleam, flames safely trammeled within glass. I sit on the edge of the bed, stroking his belly, its thick fur, its curved density. I stretch out beside him and we gaze into each other's eyes for a long, long time, listening to wild wind battering the walls. When his eyebrows arch quizzically, as if to say, *Well?*, I whisper, "Yes, Daddy Bear, this is quite the sweet surprise. You know how hot you are bound up like this."

Aidan chuckles against the bit. My stomach growls. "Your stew smells great. Hungry?"

Aidan shrugs his great shoulders. I squeeze his jock's swelling pouch. His body's clearly focused on other than food.

"I bought some really good pot. Let's get into the wine and the weed for a while, then I'll feed us. You want to eat at my feet again?"

Aidan nods. He knew I'd know what the bowl on the kitchen floor meant.

"Fine by me. Right now, though, I want to see your tattoo," I say, patting his bandaged shoulder. "All right?"

"Uh-huh," grunts Aidan.

Gently I pull the ink-smudged bandage off.

"It's beautiful," I sigh. "Fuck, Sean does such good work."

The dark blaze swirls over Aidan's muscular shoulder, sizzles down his upper arm, spills over his partially shaved left pec. Now a phoenix of frozen fire is needled into him. I press my lips to the black flame inside his skin. I suck his nipples till they're swollen and hurting, till he's pleading with me to stop. I burrow a finger up his sweaty hole, peel down his jock and suck his cock till he's groaning and trembling, just this side of spurting. Then I rise to fetch us wine and roll a joint, leaving him on the bed, humping the air, bound by his own hand, scarred by his own desire.

Together for a year. By now, it's become an art, pleasing my big bottom Bear, giving him what he wants, even when he's too ashamed to ask. Earlier tonight, it was five-alarm chili, his favorite fire-station dish, with biscuits and Bud Light, followed by cherry pie with ice cream. Now it's fire-play. "Aversion therapy," he calls it, submitting to the element most likely to end him. A gesture mixing defiance with supplication and thanks, I'd say. Last week a toppling wall almost got him.

Since we've met, I've learned how to truss the big man up, that's for sure. Tonight, balmy evening in early May, Aidan's muscle-hard arms and torso are wrapped in heavy chain. His crossed wrists are roped together in the fuzzy small of his back; a cord threaded through his thighs secures his hands to his cock and balls. He's lying on his back, his knees bent, calves pressed tightly against thighs. His feet are bound together with more chain; a very short rope cinches his ankles to the base of his ball sac. Whenever he tugs on his bonds, he only tortures his own genitals. Add to this setup the thick dildo buried in his broad butt, the alligator clamps' sharp metal teeth sunk into his nipples, the sodden bandana stuffed in his mouth, and the four strips of duct tape layered over his lips, and my slave's the helpless sacrifice he wants to be. Amazing, really: he's big enough to throw a slight guy like me through the wall, but instead he's allowed me—begged me, actually—to free him from freedom and envelop him in pure surrender. I could cut his throat right now, with one of his collectible blades, and we both know he would be in no position to stop me. The power I hold over him is the most priceless gift anyone has ever given me.

I know, dripping hot wax over his bound-up balls and blood-plump cock, that I feel something for him that I've never felt for any man before him. I know, puffing on the fat cigar he brought, blowing smoke into his face till he chokes, that I want to hold him hostage always. I know, holding the cigar's ember-heat only millimeters from his tender nipples, that I can't comprehend life without him. I know, tapping the cigar against the side of my hand again and again, covering the black mat of his chest hair with white-gray ash, rubbing the ash into his beard, smearing it on his cheeks, his nose and brow, that I need him to feel the same ardor for me.

Tonight, to commemorate our first anniversary, is the night I'm to mark Aidan as mine. We've discussed it earlier. He knows it's coming. The more he's refused to live with me, for fear of what the guys down at the fire station might think, the more he's asked for some proof of my ownership on his skin. This is why his restraints and his gag are extra-tight tonight, though there's no one in the woods surrounding this trailer to hear the screams when they come.

My cigar's a stub now, but there's enough fire left for what needs to be done. I tug on the tit-clamp chain, and Aidan growls with pain. I wipe sweat off his temples, then bend over him, raise the cigar, and ask "Are you ready? Are you sure?"

Aidan stares at me and nods for a good half-minute. His blue eyes are wider than I've ever seen them, crazed with his captivity. His face is etched with fear, longing, and awe. I hold the cigar's smoking tip an inch from his brow, as if I might brand him there. He blinks and gulps. "Roll over on your side," I say, and he does, with puffing, trussed-up difficulty.

"Move your hands," I say, and he does, hitching them up toward his shoulder blades as far as the short rope-cinch and his muscle-bound frame will allow.

"I love you." It's the first time I've said it. "Now I own you; now you'll never escape me." Aidan nods, takes a deep breath and holds it.

I touch the burning tip of the cigar to the fur-clouded small of his back. There's simultaneously a tiny hissing, the smell of burnt hair and skin, and Aidan's scream, surprisingly loud considering how thick his gag is. I lift the cigar and step back.

Aidan thrashes across the bed. The muscles of his shoulders, arms, and back bulge against his restraints. His scream gradually dwindles into sobs and then muffled cursing.

I fetch the burn ointment. I free him from bonds, gag, clamps. I anoint and bandage his wound, strip, blow out the candles, climb into bed, and hold him. "God, Bobby, it hurts bad," he moans. He rocks against me, his arms around his knees. "I love you," he moans. He's never said it before either. I stroke his thick hair and beard, his wax-sheathed dick. "Good boy, good boy," I whisper, "I'll take care of you," as if he were the young one, the small one, the one I might imprison, torture, and protect, one the indulgent years might allow me to own entirely.

Now Aidan's on his belly and I'm filling him with spit-slick, thick-girthed cock. He's wincing, chewing the pillow, begging me to screw him harder. Now the bed's scattered with broken wax, the sheets are smeared with streaks of ash, the room's saturated with the thick scents of smoke and semen.

Halfway through my second glass of port, Nathan calls. He's doing fine in D.C., attending conference sessions. He'll be home day after tomorrow. We've been together for five years; the marriage is solid, strong, likely to last. I've never told him about Aidan, about that passionate love affair fifteen years ago, about Aidan's beauty, sweetness, and submission. Nathan doesn't need to know he lives in a shadow.

Aidan died suddenly, two years into our love affair. All that time in the closet, all those years fighting fires, and he ended up dying off-duty, in a crowded gay-disco conflagration in Florida. He was visiting his retired parents in Daytona Beach, the first vacation he'd taken since I met him. According to eyewitnesses, he helped more than a dozen men escape before succumbing to the smoke. I guess his love for films focused on warriors both doomed and triumphant makes more sense in retrospect. He finally found a way to be heroic, damn him.

In D.C., Nathan hurries off to another late business dinner. In Ohio, I stand by the hearth, dripping what's left of my port on what's left of the fire. The charred crumbles smoke and hiss; I keep dripping till there's nothing but wine-soaked blackness. Tomorrow, I'll clean the fireplace, empty the ash bucket in the flowerbeds. Tomorrow, I'll twist up newspapers, crisscross kindling, and heap up logs to fire up as welcome when Nathan comes home.

Aidan was cremated. It's hard for me to imagine it: that strong, thick body; that soft, musky body hair; that swirling tribal tattoo; that scar I left in the small of his back, all consumed by flame. It's hard to imagine an inferno that hungry and hot, intense enough to swallow such strength. Since he'd been so closeted, none of his family or friends knew me, which meant—after several days of wondering how his trip was going and why he hadn't called—I read about his death in the newspaper. No one spoke to me at his funeral. He's buried back in Virginia, the pretty spruce-edged O'Neill family cemetery in Ellett Valley. There are angels and a fireman's helmet sculpted into his stone. When it rains as hard as it does tonight, I think about his ashes growing moist in black mountain earth.

Time has passed so quickly since he died. For years, I was sick with sorrow. I broke into tears when I saw a lit candle, a fire truck or firehouse. I graduated, moved to Ohio, found a job as a stage manager, met Nathan and settled down. Soon enough I'll be as old as Aidan was when we met. Soon this little bit of blond beard I've grown will shade into gray. Soon it will be December, then a new year. Soon the rains over Ohio will turn to snow, filling the brittle cornfields with white powder that grows ash gray as night descends.

From my desk drawer I lift it, the tarnished chain and padlock Aidan used to wear to please me, to signify his possession and my ownership, the slave collar he left at my trailer the last time we parted. I run my fingers over the dark stains his sweat left. Every year or so I think about burying it in the backyard, as if that gesture might help me forget him. Every year I relent, knowing it would do no good. Instead I do what I often do when Nathan is out of town: I drape the chain around my own neck, click the padlock closed, blow out the candles, and head down the hall to bed.

# COLIN AND GREGORY: 1956

Jonathan Kemp

When old men hang around public toilets while younger men piss, we aren't out for a glimpse of cock or even a grope. What roots us to the spot is the most profound feeling of envy that we cannot piss like that anymore. It's a mark of respect. When you reach fifty, it trickles.

He pisses like a horse. I can hear him through the whole house. It's not a big house—he calls it the doll's house—and he is forever banging his head on my lampshades and doorjambs, while I totter behind him like a puppy. He strides through my tiny rooms with such confidence and familiarity, as if it were a castle and he its prince; I feel in comparison like the valet who can call nothing here his own.

When I first saw him about a month ago, I thought him quite the handsomest boy I'd seen in a long time. When he removed his clothing, I saw what I had been missing in a model: someone who shone more when he was nude than clothed. Skin with light trapped beneath it. Skin that looked complete rather than exposed. That looked painted, full of color and life, blood blue and flesh pink. Yellows, purples, whites. Tints I didn't know I could ever reproduce. He is more relaxed when naked, more himself, more at home in his flesh than his clothes. And because of that you don't really notice he is naked.

He has a masculine grace that is best expressed by the word noble. There is something classical about him; his proportion and bearing suggest Michelangelo's *David* come to life, if that doesn't sound too grand. He speaks with the jagged edges of simplicity, and whilst that is not without its charm, it is clear that the sophistication of his being is concentrated on the surface.

I fill acres of paper with his crouched figure, his legs bent and twisted beyond recognition, his spine an abacus, a string of pearls arching impossibly as he nearly swallows himself like Ouroboros. There is nothing that he will not do, no inch of flesh so sacred to him it cannot be splayed and displayed to my gaze. The damp, dark caves of his armpits. The taut plateau of his belly. The smoothed edges of his muscular buttocks, carved to Hellenic perfection—if I placed my tongue there, I should expect them to be cold and hard as marble. The masculine sweep from his hairline to the right angle of his shoulder as fluid and mesmerizing as any waterfall. The line of gravity that runs the length of his torso, from the hollow of his throat to the jewel of his navel, cruciformed by the stigmata of his nut brown nipples. The pucker of his anus like a knot in a tree. How does he feel, spread out before me? How can he not feel shame, I wonder. Yet nothing he does or says suggests he feels it.

After he left today, I walked into the bathroom and looked at myself in the mirror and muttered like an incantation the words *You are old*, the distance granted by the second person address in no way diminishing the painful truth of that statement. His presence diminishes me; I am wracked with envy that I am not him. They say desire and identification are almost indistinguishable, but I never understood this till I met him. I stood naked before the mirror, something I have not done since the years of curiosity adolescence entails. I looked at my reflection, at my rounded, narrow shoulders with their tufts of gray hair, my rotund belly, my shriveled privates, my legs like white sticks, and I felt a deep sadness.

I cannot recall what it felt like to be young. I suppose that is because I was too busy being young to think about it, to store it for future reference. Perhaps that is why, as Wilde said, youth is wasted on the young. Or perhaps because my youth does not in actuality warrant recollection. Perhaps it was a nonevent. But I must have been a youth at some stage in my life, all things considered. I must have been in some sense flawless and innocent. Photographs must supply some clue. Another face stares back at me, though, from the few I do possess, never having liked to have my picture taken. I look at a stranger whose passions and fears are irretrievable now. Christ, and I'm only fifty-five.

He came over again today. I should stop saying "he." He has a name. But it is such a grotesque name I fail to link it with him, with his beauty: Gregory. There's no nobility in it, no grace. It sounds like the death rattle of an ancient bullfrog. He told me his friends call him Gore, and since this is the name of a novelist whose books I enjoy, I feel happier calling him that. Gore has a nobility that more closely matches the patrician stature of his presence.

He's not shy at all and strips off as soon as he's in the studio. Just stands and disrobes. I usually offer a bathrobe and get them to undress before coming into the studio, but he has none of that. It's as if he can't wait to be naked, as if that is his natural state and clothes are an encumbrance. I look at him and praise the good fortune that allows me to witness the sight of him naked.

We start off with a few short poses to warm up and then move to longer ones. He does not fidget like some of the models I've had. We chat as I sketch.

His parents are gypsies—or, as he prefers to call them, traveling people. His mother is French and his father Italian, and he is fluent in both languages, as well as English, having been born here, outside Brighton. He left his parents at the age of sixteen and traveled the world on merchant ships, worked in circuses, on building sites, occasionally whoring. I accept this revelation with a worldly nod, as if I meet renters every day, though inside I am shocked and excited. I wanted to bombard him with questions but beneath his apparent openness he is remarkably guarded.

"Do you find your work interesting?" I say.

He says it gives him plenty of money and sex and saves him from having to work.

He seems to know exactly what he is doing, and why; and I, for one, cannot stand in judgment. I am plagued with questions, having had so little physical pleasure and placed so little value on it. I want to know what it is like to give and take pleasure in that way, to live outside normal society so gleefully and shamelessly. I want to know what it is like to be so fearless.

I ask none of these questions and continue to draw in silence.

"Most of the models who pose for the group do it," he says at last, and I know I am expected to pick this up as a topic of conversation.

"And does it pay well?" I ask.

"I made ten bob from one fella last week."

"He must have been well off."

"A don from Cambridge. You know what he wanted me to do?"

"What?"

"He wanted me to sit down on his face." He is grinning.

"Clothed or unclothed?" I have never spoken of such things with another human being in my life.

"Unclothed. I had to rub my arse in his face while he played with me. And the whole time he's trying to speak, but his words are being muffled by my arse. Then I spilt onto his belly."

I am looking at him by now, my hand stilled, struck dumb by this image he has conjured. I am not at all certain what I might say at this point. I am ill-equipped for this.

"It was all over in twenty minutes and he hands me a fiver. That's the most I ever had."

"And will you see him again?" I ask, sounding like a maiden aunt discussing courtship prospects.

"I hope to see him again," he says with a smile that seems to invite something I can barely recognize.

Long after he has gone I am plagued by the image of him crushing his behind into a man's face. I cannot sleep for imagining it.

Once a month on a Friday afternoon for the past year I have been attending a local life-drawing group run by a friendly old woman with the kind of scatterbrain so characteristic of those members of the aristocracy who have fallen foul of the arts, or "living *la vie de Bohème,*" as she puts it. Miss Wilkes is a retired arts mistress from one of the private girls' schools in the Home Counties. She treats us like schoolgirls. There are five of us, all middle-aged men or older, and all, I imagine, of the same persuasion as myself. Maurice wears rouge and calls everybody "dear." Kenneth is a retired navigator from the Royal Navy who stands incredibly close to the male models during the tea break, cornering them so they are obliged to listen to him drone on and on about his life at sea. Malcolm is the most verbally explicit. He has a code for rating the standard of the male models' backsides. The ones he likes best he calls "Harrods." He does tiny, cramped watercolors—two to a page of his small sketchbook—and sucks on his paintbrush, making a repulsive sound and ending up with a black tongue. Peter, like me, hardly says a word.

Gore came to model for the group about a month ago. During the tea break I found myself arranging for him to model for me privately. I have done this occasionally with models from the group, though none came more than once or twice. They are unreliable, and not being local boys, are often reluctant to travel so far out of town for so little money.

I had been trying without success to recall who it is Gore reminds me of, for there is something familiar about him I cannot quite place. And it finally came to me today, as I was drawing, as I focused on that face and body. He is the spitting image of a young boy I met thirty years ago, under the following circumstances. After leaving college at twenty-one, I worked for four years at an advertising studio in Regent Street run by an acquaintance of my father's—Frank Symonds. On this particular occasion I had been assigned a job that involved drawing the male figure. It was a catalog of some description, a men's clothing catalog. During the briefing, Symonds told me he thought I should brush up on my figure drawing. He asked me to stay behind after work, and arranged for a model to come round whom I was to draw for a couple of hours whilst he did some paperwork.

Trevor was a beautiful young man, tall, broad shouldered, with black hair and green eyes. Symonds took us down to a storeroom in the basement, where he had set up some angle-poise lamps and cushions. The room was cold. My heart raced at the prospect of this boy disrobing before me, feeling no concern for his possible discomfort, I must admit. Symonds and the lad were clearly familiar, and they joked while Trevor removed his clothes. "I'll try and locate a heater," Symonds said, "otherwise your shivering will be most distracting." Symonds looked at me and said, "Don't worry, it gets bigger," and gave a wink before leaving. It was a side of him I had not seen before, slightly effeminate, repulsive, in thrall to this.

"Where do you want me, guv?"

I found my mouth dry and had to swallow before replying.

"Just stand over there to begin with," I muttered, pointing to a pool of light between the two lamps.

He stood stock-still, arms behind his back, legs slightly apart, feet firmly set on the floor, looking into the far left-hand corner behind me.

"This do?"

"Perfect," I stammered, sitting down and grabbing my paper and pencils with sweaty hands.

Symonds came back, carrying a three-bar electric fire, which he plugged into a socket and aimed in Trevor's direction. "This'll ensure it doesn't shrink to nothing, eh, lad?" he chuckled, before turning to me. "Fine figure of a man, isn't he? Such stature. He should be cast in bronze, don't you think?"

"Yes," I said, looking down at the blank sheet on my knee. "Perfect."

Symonds stared openly at the young man's genitals. "Anyway," he chirped, dragging his gaze away reluctantly. "You've got him for two hours, so make the most of him. I'll be upstairs should you need me."

I don't know whether those first drawings were any good. I'm sure they weren't. I seem to remember spending long stretches of time drinking in that body, my hand making random marks on the paper that bore little resemblance to the vision before me. Every time I looked at him I wanted to thank God for creating such beauty, and for allowing me to witness its sublime splendor.

At one point he got an erection and laughed off an apology.

"No, no, it's fine, don't worry about it," I said breathlessly.

Every evening after work for the next two weeks Symonds would present me with a different boy, but it is Trevor's ash white body and crow black hair, Trevor's pale tan nipples and pale green eyes, that are the indelible memory of that time. I never saw him again. I drew ten different young men in as many days, and yet only that first one registers with me now. The others, beautiful as they were, have faded, so that Trevor's has become the face and body I attribute to each of them. He has, I suppose, delineated my desire.

Looking at Gore this morning was like looking back across the years and seeing Trevor, the same green eyes and boxer's nose, the same angle of the shoulders, even the same pucker to the foreskin, from beneath which that cyclopean eye stares out to assess me like a wary animal.

Gore has done very little "proper" work in his life. A few short-term jobs as an office boy or general dogsbody, work that never lasted; his temperament is such that the minute he felt he'd had enough, he resigned, using the money he had earned to travel. He studied yoga and meditation in Tibet, rope work in North Africa, Noh theater in Japan, picked grapes in Italy, smuggled drugs in and out of just about everywhere. He spent an evening with a group of Arabs in the middle of a desert outside Morocco, conversing through the only Arab who spoke French. Having chatted underneath a star-flecked sky on a myriad of topics, smoking hashish and drinking wine with them all evening, he was told that they were all about to indulge in a homosexual orgy, and he was welcome to stay or be driven to the nearest town. He chose to stay, of course.

I cannot begin to explain what inadequacies his stories provoke in me, nor what inspiration his very presence works on my art. I feel this peculiar mixture of desire and regret, disgust and fascination, and these feelings seem to spill into the images that appear when I draw. Even as he makes me recognize the narrowness of my life, I feel freer than I have ever felt. There's an urgency in my work that I've never known before, a tension that expresses itself in the most ambiguous and intriguing ways. These new sketches look like nothing I've ever seen.

I remember sitting in my father's library as a small boy and poring over volumes of Hellenic statuary. The eroticism of them was potent to me. I had seen men naked at swim, and relished the furtive sight, but the poetry of the marble was electric. I could openly stare at reproductions of Renaissance paintings and statues for hours, transfixed by something I couldn't quite express, a feeling in the gullet that was more than visceral, a humility and awe, a sense of disbelief that human hands were responsible for this divinity of forms. I associated it, when I got older and studied the work of Immanuel Kant, with the notion of the sublime. Something in excess of human understanding. But I also came to recognize its presence in the emotion we call desire—in my experience of desire, at least. I first masturbated over a photograph of Bernini's sculpture of Antaeus and Hercules.

When I was about ten, I took a sheet of paper and a pencil and tried to copy a sketch by Leonardo. It was an appalling scribble, but I started again, and over time, over many weeks, something emerged, some movement of the wrist that enabled me to capture a faint semblance of the original. I did it over and over, till I could draw the thing without looking at the original, by simply concentrating on a point of light that seemed to dance like a star on the tip of the pencil, like a spark created by its contact with the paper. The sketch by Leonardo represented the musculature of a man, and its erotic charge, whilst not something I could in any sense articulate at that age, seems to me now not insignificant. Art gave me the opportunity to feast my eyes on naked men.

# THE BED FROM CRAIGSLIST

Rob Wolfsham

A guy from Craigslist fucked me.

I didn't even meet him through the personals. I told myself I'd never hook up with a guy that way, but this was a special case. I had just moved into a house—my first house after living in the dorms for two years. I had packed my entire life into the back of my Chevy Blazer and said peace to my weird potluck roommates. Leaving transient dorm life, I had no furniture to my name.

"You have to go to Craigslist," Kolby said as we stared at my new empty room. "People sell cheap shit on there all the time."

Two garbage bags were stuffed into a corner with four boxes of books and a laptop case, with a Canadian flag draped on top—my entire life. Kolby's one of two new roommates. We've been friends since freshman year. He's straight but he knows about me. This was his first house too so we had a shared giddiness about it all.

"I can't get something on Craigslist," I said.

"Why not?"

"It's weird. I don't trust it."

"Dude, you see this I'm wearing?"

I glanced at Kolby's teal T-shirt, tight against his fat. The band name Boards of Canada was spelled across his chest in a yellow font under simple icon art of lollipop trees and a building.

"Craigslist," he punctuated. "A roadie was selling all his shit. I got it for like three bucks."

"Do you even know who that band is?"

He looked down, stupidly pulling on the shirt, blond hair falling into his face and bushy red beard. "Yeah. They're like this cool Canadian punk band that's touring—"

"They're from Scotland. They do electronic music."

"Why do you always have to make me feel stupid?"

I surveyed my room. "I need to figure something out, before I have to sleep."

"Dude, just sleep on the couch," Kolby said. "At least until you get some sort of bed."

"I'm getting something tomorrow." We had moved furniture into the living room and I was beat, tired and achy. I needed a shower.

My room had its own connecting bathroom. Kolby and Derrick shared the one in the hall. It was sort of this unspoken thing that I got the room with the bathroom—my own bathroom. I'm actually not sure why. I mean, I guess it was because I'm gay and they kind of treated bathroom territory as if I'm a girl. Don't get me wrong, I'm one of the guys to them. Just little things reminded me that I wasn't entirely the same. Or who knows, maybe it was simply because of physical difference. Kolby and Derrick are both big guys. I'm dainty compared to them. Derrick is a six-foot-four, two-hundred-pound man-wall:

black hair buzzed, electric cyan eyes, Roman nose, former Army ROTC guy. But, thank god, he quit just before his twenty-first birthday.

I wasn't going to turn twenty-one for another couple of months, but alcohol wasn't a problem. Derrick and Kolby always made sure our house was stocked.

I knew we were going to make an odd household. Kolby is a libertarian neckbeard. I'm a tree-loving faggot. Derrick is a red-state, gun-loving conservative. But there are nuances about him. He's not a homophobe. Never was. And he wanted the war to end too.

Kolby left my room to continue unpacking. I showered. That night we ordered pizza, drank beer and watched "Arrested Development" on a TV sitting on the living room's hardwood floor. None of us had a TV stand or entertainment center. Mountains of plastic bags surrounded the couch. We subscribed to the philosophy of storing everything in Wal-Mart sacks.

Aside from moving, it had been a lazy July with no class in sight for weeks.

After we finished a third episode around one A.M., Kolby went to his room. His bed was already set up. Derrick had a bed, but it was still in pieces and he was too tired to put it together, so he slept with me on the couch.

He's secure with himself. We slept feet to face anyway. Since he's much taller than me, I rested my face against his fuzzy calves with my ass against the crotch of his boxer-briefs. He absentmindedly put his arm around my shins. I tolerated temptation, somehow.

In the morning, Derrick went to work at Papa Georgie Pizza. Kolby smoked a bowl, which I helped with, then he fried a stupid amount of bacon. Kolby didn't have a job except making the house smell like schwag and pork.

"Are you going to Wal-Mart for furniture?" Kolby asked. His greasy blond locks stuck to his face.

"Yeah I think so, I'll let you know."

He turned on the old Nintendo, blowing and coughing into game cartridges to get them to work. I went to my room and sat on the Berber carpet with my laptop.

I searched the Wal-Mart website—everything was shit. I typed in *craigslist.com*—just to look.

The minimalist link-riddled page loaded. The little category *men seeking men* stuck out like a tranny in a church, but I ignored it.

I clicked *furniture* and waded through bullshit: lots of entries for sectional couches, kids' furniture, desks and chairs, even a church pew. I was reminded how much I hate Lubbock. I didn't see any beds under *Tues July 06* so I moved down to *Mon July 05*. Nothing there either. I scrolled to the bottom. There were some beds, but all kings and canopies, for hundreds of dollars I don't have.

I gave up and looked at random disgusting XTube videos for twenty minutes. I found one video of a guy sticking an entire horse dildo up his ass. I felt better about myself. When I went back to Craigslist and checked the furniture section, voila, I found at the top: *Queen Sized Mattress and Bed Frame!!!!! $90.*

The entry said it included a mattress protector too, which the picture proved.

I looked around at my empty room again. I had to act quickly: I was in an awesome new house yet living like a garbage bag gypsy. I called the number.

A woman with a thick Southern drawl answered. "Yes, who is this?"

"Yeah hi, I uh—" I cringed and moved to sit cross-legged on the floor. "I'm calling about your Craigslist posting."

A male in the background yelled, "Who is that?" with even more drawl.

"I don't know," she said. "It's a girl named Craig."

"No," I tried to say. "Craigslist. And I'm a guy."

"Craigliss," she echoed.

"Give me that," his voice approached angrily. "Who is this?"

"I'm Travis. I'm calling about the bed you put on Craigslist," I said as quick and clear as possible.

"Well all right, I just put that up there," he said pleased and surprised.

"Yeah, I saw. I moved into a house and have no furniture, so I'm a little desperate." I grabbed my hair in irritation. Why did I tell him that?

"Good deal, good deal, man," he said, calm and smooth.

"Yeah—"

"Yeah," he said.

Awkward.

"I've never done this," I said. "Do I come to your house or something?"

The guy was silent for a moment. "Yeah," he said. "Come on by. Take a look at the bed. If you like what you see, we can do business."

He gave me his address, which I Google-mapped. He lived about three miles away on the outskirts of town: "Turn left at the Ford dealership," his twang echoed in my head. He told me to come in thirty minutes. I showered and put on cargo shorts and a red-and-white-stripped polo that was tight on my skinny frame.

I was nervous on the drive. I had that same pounding heart I get when I know I'm about to do something with a guy.

The one-story house sat in front of a vast cotton field with a garage and a covered driveway. The paint on the wood paneling was peeling like cracked desert earth. A Medusa of vines sprawled over the white picket fence surrounding the front yard. The house had no neighbors on either side, just dusty lots where the cotton rows tapered off.

As I parked my Blazer, a Ford Taurus was backing out of the driveway, a woman driving. I got out of my car and she saw me. I waved. She didn't. The day was overcast and unseasonably cool for July in West Texas.

A black Ford F-150 sat in the covered driveway, jacked up. Amber light glowed from the open garage door. A lanky body in a grease-smeared wifebeater and jeans lay sprawled under the truck. I could only see his torso, spread legs, and bare dirty feet.

A grease monkey. Great.

I could see the queen-sized mattress sitting upright in the cluttered garage.

I strolled slowly up to the truck, pulling at my fingers. "Excuse me," I said politely.

His power wrench whirred every few seconds. His wifebeater inched up his taut white stomach, revealing a coarse, black happy trail. I got down on my knees at the end of the truck, peering with my head sideways.

We made eye contact. He jolted upward, almost face-planting the axle. He pulled earbud headphones out of his ears. His iPod, or whatever it was, blasted tinny rock music that I could hear from several feet away. He rolled himself out from under the truck.

"Are you—?" He stood up: six feet tall, lanky with black greasy hair. He had a two-part trash 'stache under his nose, muttonchop sideburns, and stubble. He had ghostly light-green eyes. He looked young, maybe in his midtwenties. He pulled down his dirty wifebeater, erasing the view of his trail and lack of a belt.

"Yeah, I'm the guy," I said. "From Craigslist." I looked elsewhere, like I had just said something dirty.

He tossed a dirty rag into his left hand and extended his right with a grin, "I'm Joe."

I looked at the sooty hand.

He looked at his hand and quickly started wiping it. "Oh, sorry there, I guess we don't have to shake."

"It's okay," I said. "I'm Travis." I made a dumb wave. Yes, I waved to someone standing two feet in front of me.

"Yeah, I put that bed over there on the Internet and wasn't expecting much," he said as if we were already talking about it. "But you called lightning quick."

Texan accents are funny with the letter *I*. Get a Texan to say, "Friday night lights." You'll know what I mean. I can't really complain. I made the decision to come to this West Texas college town instead of going to school in Dallas.

Joe wasn't bad looking. He was actually attractive. I was surprised to think so because of his trash 'stache and overall filthiness.

"Can I see it?" I asked.

"See what?"

"The bed."

"Oh, yeah, right this way, sir." He gestured to the open garage. Sickly yellow light filtered through the dusty air. The garage was cluttered with furniture, shelves, cabinets, birdhouses, and tools. The brilliant white mattress stood out in all the wood.

I was having second thoughts. I was going to be sleeping on this thing and I didn't like its current environment. But it *was* zipped into a plastic mattress protector.

Joe waded over to the mattress and started pulling it out of the garage, almost frantically. He was nervous. Though he was wiry, with tight arm muscle, the mattress was almost too much for him, until he managed to yank it up and over some boxes. The box spring and bed frame slid down and clattered against shelves. He unzipped the protector. "Come get a look and see what you think," he huffed.

I climbed over boxes to get next to him. The mattress looked spotless.

"Only six months old," he said. "It belongs to my brother, who moved up to Michigan for law school. He was using my garage for storage and now that he's gone I wanna get rid of all his shit so I can have my garage back."

"Cool."

"So you like it? Wanna make a deal?"

"Ninety dollars, right?"

"Yeah, unless you had another price in mind."

I didn't want to bargain. I didn't know how. It didn't matter, a queen-sized bed ran for at least two hundred in most stores, so this was a steal. "That's fine." I scratched the back of my neck.

Two moths fought over the yellow light above, darting into each other.

"I can't take it now," I said. "I have to get my friend with a truck to come get it. I drive that Chevy Blazer."

"Oh, that?" Joe stepped around to the open garage door to get a look at my shitty brown SUV parked in front of the mailbox. "What is that, a two-thousand?"

"Two-thousand one."

"Had any problems with the heater block?"

"It was just replaced."

"Yup." He nodded knowingly. "Next is going to be the balls."

"The what?"

"The ball joints. They connect the suspension."

"Right, yeah. One actually collapsed just two months ago."

"That's what's happening with those, around this time. Like clockwork."

He knew his shit.

"That's kind of like wine isn't it?" I laughed a little.

He stared blankly.

"You know. Wine. It ages and can change..." My voice drifted away. I wiped my face. "I was going twenty when the suspension collapsed. The tow truck driver said if I was on the freeway, I would have flipped."

He patted my shoulder. "Well, praise the Lord you're all right."

The mention of "the Lord" annoyed me as much as his hand dirtying my polo shirt.

"I'm all done with my truck right here," he said. "I can take the bed over to your place."

"No. That's nice of you, but I don't want to put you through the trouble."

"You're paying me," he said. "You seem like a nice guy, a normal guy. I was all iffy about the Internet, but you're all right." He nodded with his chin up, smiling thinly like he was pleased with himself.

I said nothing and glanced at the clutter around me.

"So you just moved into a new house?" he asked.

"Yeah," I said. "Yesterday."

"You a Tech student?"

"Yeah, I'm going to be a junior."

"I went to Tech," he said, looking past me. "Didn't last long. What are you studying?"

"Creative writing."

His eyebrows went up. "Neat. That's different. Really neat—writing."

Mmm, wake up and smell the bullshit.

"My wife graduated in journalism," he said.

His wife. I noticed the wedding band on his ring finger.

"Cool. Do you want to just follow my car?" I asked. "To my house?"

"Yeah, yeah. So we got a deal." He slapped his palms together. Soot puffed away. "Here, help me get this in my truck." He tugged on the mattress.

I helped. Not really. I'm a weakling, but I helped tie it down, pulling ropes taut against the mattress like it was a Shibari victim.

"This is my baby," he said, patting the gate of the truck bed: the ass of the car. "Hey, did you need any other furniture since you just moved in?" He dashed into his garage. "Cabinet? TV stand?" He pointed at each item in his flea market.

"I really just have money for the bed."

"No, I mean just have it. I want to get rid of my brother's shit pronto. I want my garage back, you know what I mean?"

"For free?"

"Need a wine rack?" He picked one up. "You said you like wine, right?"

I smiled tightly, forcing it into a frown. "I'll take the TV stand maybe."

"It's yours." He pulled out the short pinewood stand with a shelf for a DVD player and cubbies on each side for whatever else. His bony arms held it up over his head. "I'll just throw it in the back of the truck."

He tossed in the wine rack anyway along with a laundry hamper and a small bookshelf. "Because I'm sure you got tons of books to go with that wine," he said.

"Thanks." I looked away, fighting my tendency to blush. I did have books, so many I used to use a microwave for storage.

With everything set I got in my car and headed home; his big black Ford pickup followed.

Joe was a stranger, I realized, and I was taking him to my house. I checked my rearview mirror every five seconds. He talked on a phone the whole way. We drove by campus and into my neighborhood. I lived in the heart of town a few blocks from the university.

In the driveway we unloaded the TV stand, hamper, bookshelf, and wine rack.

The large living room window facing the front lawn had OBAMA neatly painted on the glass in big blue letters with MCCAIN underneath.

"What the hell?" Joe asked in a sharp drawl, *hell* twisting into *hill*.

"The people who lived here before," I explained quickly. "Two girls. One liked Obama. One liked McCain, so they had both. We're thinking of keeping it since I'm voting Obama, but my roommate Derrick is in the can for McCain."

Joe scratched his armpit. "You think he's got a chance?"

"Who Obama? Absolutely."

"I don't know." He paused, delicately finding his words. "I just think him—a black guy—if he gets it, I give it two months before some redneck..." He lifted his arms and squinted one eye, miming a sniper rifle, shaking his arms in a faux recoil.

I grew angry. "If Bush hasn't been assassinated, I think Obama will be fine."

Joe laughed. "Maybe."

I didn't sense he was racist; his tone was pity, which could be patronizingly racist anyway.

I noticed Kolby's car was gone as we carried the TV stand into the house. He was probably off buying bud.

"Nice house," Joe said inside. "Nice hardwood floors."

The living room was still a mess with all the Wal-Mart bags, but under the clutter it was spacious. The walls were painted deep red. Joe tried to look into the den that had a fireplace. He set the TV on the stand and brought in the hamper and wine rack, adding them to the disorder. He took the bookshelf to my room.

"You do need furniture," he said. "Where do you want the bed?"

I stood in the far corner of my room. "Long-ways here."

He brought in the frame and started latching pieces together.

"Really, you don't have to do this," I said. "I can set it up. Or my roommates can help."

"My treat," he said, not looking at me.

His dirty hands and greasy wifebeater stuck out in my clean bare room. I could smell his worked body, the gripping salty musk of his underarms. The frame was set and I helped him carry the box spring and mattress in. I thought I pulled something in my arm but ignored the pain as we slid the box spring in place on the frame. Panting together, we toppled the mattress onto the box spring. Wood clattered on metal and the springs hissed.

Everything was adjusted until perfect: my bed, nuzzled in the dark corner of the room. We stared at the pristine white mattress covered in a plastic protector. "You got any sheets yet?" he asked, huffing, but he hadn't cracked a sweat.

I wiped my sweaty forehead with my forearm. I couldn't remember the last time I had broken a sweat. "Not yet," I said. "I've never had a queen. Do you want a beer? We keep our house pretty stocked."

"Yeah, I'll take a beer." He sighed, sitting on my new bed, plastic crinkling. "What you got?"

"Tecate, Dos Equis, Shiner Bock, Coors Light..."

"Give me a Coors."

Of course he would pick Coors.

I went to the kitchen, opened the fridge and grabbed myself a Tecate with his Coors. I stared into the cold humming air and silently screamed *What the fuck am I doing?*

I returned to my room, which was now slightly more furnished and inviting.

Joe sat on the bed, rubbing his shoulder, scratching it with dirty fingernails. I handed him the beer and sat close on his right, plastic crinkling. He gulped from the can.

"So you fix cars for a living?" I asked.

"Yeah," he exhaled. "I work in a shop out on Highway Eighty-four. My wife works at the paper, so she helps pay the bills too, but who knows how long that'll last."

"No one reads anymore." I sipped my beer.

"What do you do?" he asked. "Just a student?"

"Yeah. I like to think I am sort of a writer."

"Why sort of? You either are or aren't."

"I haven't published much, just some poems."

"You're a poet," he said.

"Actually no," I said. "I want to do fiction, novel writing. The poetry happened because of a class I took."

"Got a poem you can read?" he asked like it was a rabbit I could pull out of a hat.

My shoulders seized up.

"C'mon, read a poem," he said.

I looked at him. He grinned mischievously, flashing crooked teeth. He didn't give a shit about poetry. He was patronizing me. Then again, I didn't give a shit about poetry either. His ghostly green eyes had a spark of curiosity. He probably hadn't heard a poem read out loud to him before.

I gave in and slid off the bed down to the floor where my laptop slept. On my knees, I pulled it open. My desktop background flickered on.

Shit.

A shirtless built redhead stared out of the screen, standing on a beach, framed in icons. I almost slammed the laptop shut, but figured it was too late.

"Nice picture," Joe said flatly, his voice looming from the bed behind me.

"Yeah, my laptop is sort of private."

"It's cool, man. I kinda got a sense you were fruity."

I stared at the wall ahead and should have felt insulted, but in his beer-soothed voice, it came out odd and neutral. Blood rushed to my cheeks like I just ate a habanero. I didn't turn to look at him. He swallowed two more gulps of beer.

I stared down at my shirt. "Do you still want to hear a poem?"

"Yeah," he said in that slow drawl, yearning.

I took a moment to choose one, then opened it and jumped in:

> "*Highway Flirt—by Travis McCreedy.*
>
> "*You're the turn and wink, the freeway eye-contact, two lanes over, cars like zoetropes. You recline, still, in the rapid blinking eye of traffic and tollbooth jingling, wrist flicks of light caught into your fingers threading into sun swallowed tunnels. Look at me from over the brim of your titanium blue steed. Wind rushes hotly away like sine wave ghosts. Every trip comes to an end. We can pull over. Resist the event horizon where not even lust can escape—*"

Hands grabbed my shoulder blades, clenching fistfuls of my polo shirt, pulling it tight. The poem fizzled away as I pushed against his knuckles and clawed at the denim knees coming around both sides of me.

His hands shifted to clench around my chest. I grinded back into his bony body. His warm breath exhaled unevenly against my neck. He swallowed and kissed my neck, dragging wet lips to my left earlobe. One hand grabbed my thigh and scooped up my cargo shorts to my crotch, getting a fistful of my boxer-loose balls and dick. He stunk like man and his breath quivered into my ear. He squeezed my dick through my shorts. He shoved against my ass and his arm trembled around my chest.

He kneaded my pecs, slow and repetitive, unsure where to go. I put my palms on his knuckles to still them. One hand snuck under the brim of my shorts, snatching at my dick. Stunned, I pushed him back against the bed. He pulled an arm around my chest and yanked me back onto the mattress in one long clumsy drag.

I fell on his chest while his hand groped under my boxers, tugging and grasping my dick. My shoulder dug into his neck. He strained for air. I fumbled at his waist, trying to slip my hands under, but his jeans were tight against pale skin. He pulled my hands off him, then yanked my cargo shorts down to my knees, along with my boxers. My six-inch cock was exposed to the air. He stroked it slowly, methodically, almost mechanically.

"Faster," I moaned.

He didn't change speed, as if he couldn't hear me through the fog of gay lust. His other hand tugged at my balls—a little too rough. I writhed against him and moaned again. My shoulder choked his neck and he slid out from under me and turned me on my side. He spooned me and jacked me off and pressed his forehead to the back of my neck. He bucked the crotch of his jeans into my exposed ass in a slow grind, like a pumpjack.

It drove me nuts. "Take them off," I said quickly.

He sat up and pulled his shirt off, clumsy and shaking. He stripped on his knees until he was naked. The hot breathing stench of his body made my cock stiffen and drip precum on the plastic mattress protector. His seven-inch cut dick stood perfectly straight, pale with a bright pink head.

I lay back and he crawled over me and stared down at me with a look of fear and uncertainty. My fingers grazed his throbbing cock, tickling the head and the underside.

He looked down at my uncut dick and stroked it again, playing with the foreskin as it rolled over the cockhead, smearing precum, lubing his palm.

"I want..." he started, rasping for air. "I want to fuck you." He found his beer and downed the rest with his elbow in the air, head tilted back, Adam's apple on his scraggly neck sliding up and down with each gulp.

I told him where to find a condom and lube.

He knew how to handle the condom, but I smeared lube all over his sheathed dick. Instinct kicked in and he crawled over me. I lay back and lifted my legs in the air and rested them on his shoulders, presenting my hairless pink hole to his dick. He kept looking up at my eyes as he pushed his dick against my hole, harder and harder, hesitating as if he wasn't sure he was doing it right. My hole gave way, his cockhead slipping in. I arched off the bed and he slid his cock in past a pulsing tight barrier.

"Boy, shit." He stretched his jaw out, head arching back, looking at the ceiling. "So fucking tight," he rasped.

His cock was buried almost to the base, head so far in I felt like I'd piss. I grabbed his bony forearms and my fingers dragged up to his wiry biceps. I dropped my legs around his sides to his waist.

A hand grabbed my hip and the other clutched my shoulder,

his wedding ring cool and painful. He curved back, dick sliding out just to the edge of its head. I moaned with the hot slide. He pressed his lips together, face furrowing, and shoved in deeper, drunk on the discovery of tight warm muscles around his dick. I stroked myself, hard and aching. He fucked slowly, savoring each lube-greased inch, each undulation seconds long, labored and transfixed. I flexed my insides around his invading maleness, making my own my cock bounce. "God damn," he muttered.

"Fuck me like you would fuck some bitch," I said.

He picked up the pace and swished his hips, his happy trail slapping my balls. He grabbed my hips. With my legs still wrapped around him, his forearms clenched around my thighs, pressing them tight against his ribs.

He looked at me, panting with his mouth open in a ghostly zombie stare. I thought he would drool on me as he fucked.

"You feel so good," he moaned in his twang, and slammed his hips into me until he was a jackrabbit fucking me. My moans shook with each slam. The *V* of his torso spanked my thighs.

He stared now at the wall, lips pinched with an underbite like he was furious. "Fuck I'm close," he strained. I clutched his bony ass with one hand, pinching his tight hairy cheek, pulling it into me as I jacked myself. His dick sailed past my prostate, each piston pump shooting pleasure from my insides to my balls. His sweaty palms grabbed the sides of my face, fingers pushing into my hair as he pounded and groaned. I tightened my legs around him and tightened my ass for him and pumped my dick. He growled to the ceiling and lunged into me and twisted his dick deep inside. It pulsed and throbbed against the walls of my rectum, against my prostate, each pulse feeding into mine. I cried out as my cum spurted onto my stomach and hand. My rectum choked his dick. He pumped into my ass, slapping skin, groaning loudly and painfully, as if he were being shot.

The door of the room burst open. Derrick was running in, head forward like a battering ram. He screeched to a stop halfway to the bed and seized up at the sight of my feet in the air, hairy asscheeks pounding into me.

Joe was still cumming. He looked back at Derrick and groaned, "Shit! Shit!"

"Derrick! Get out!" I screamed.

"Holy shit," Derrick said, stepping back. "Fuck. Shit. Sorry." He realized he was staring. He grabbed his face and stumbled out of the room, nearly tripping over a garbage bag. He slammed the door shut.

Joe yanked his dick from my ass so fast it popped out. My body flinched. He stood by the bed and peeled the condom from his dick.

"Wait, wait, it's okay," I tried to soothe. "It was just my roommate."

"Where do I put this, man?" he asked, holding up the condom half-filled with cum. "Where do I put this?"

I paused for a second, momentarily impressed by the volume of his solid white spunk. But I didn't have a trash can. Just a bed.

"Put it on the floor," I said, exhausted by his sudden fear and total discomfort with being here with me.

He dropped it on the floor and wiped his hand on the plastic bed, then scooped up his jeans and wifebeater. He slid the jeans on without underwear and yanked the wifebeater on, muttering, "I gotta go." He rushed to the door, kicking a beer can by accident. He wasn't drunk. Just hungover on gay.

I slipped my boxers on and ran after him. Derrick stood in the hallway and Joe dashed past him. Derrick looked at me like a vulture in the headlights, me, his skinny half-naked gay roommate running after a guy. This was a new visual for him. My gayness had been discussed, not witnessed.

"Joe," was all I could say as the grease monkey ran barefoot across dead yellow grass to the driveway. He leapt into his truck and put on a trucker cap and roared out of the driveway, skidding down the street.

"Dude," Derrick said behind me, startling me. "I am so sorry."

I pinched the bridge of my nose. The engine of Joe's truck roared into the distance over the summer-hail battered roofs of our neighborhood. "It's fine," I said.

"I ruined it didn't I?" Derrick asked in the most gentle voice I'd ever heard from his tall beefy body.

I looked up at him and sighed. "Actually no, you were too late."

"Hey...dude?" His falcon nose was aimed at my crotch, velvet blue eyes smirking.

"What?" I asked, stepping back.

"We're roommates and all now, and really close friends—but you have cum on you."

I looked down. A splatter of cum was dripping down my happy trail to my boxers. I covered it with my fumbling hand, which was also drenched in cum.

Derrick started laughing, "Dude, I...I can't stand here and look at this."

I was so embarrassed. I ran to my room and hopped in the shower, washing myself for a good twenty minutes while pondering the hot dicking I had just gotten. Out of the shower, I wrapped a blue towel around myself and stared at the new bed. The plastic mattress protector was crinkled up in wild patterns from the movement of our bodies. I realized I never paid Joe the money for the bed.

I thought to call him right away, but had a feeling he wouldn't answer. I sent him an email: *Joe, I still owe you ninety bucks.* I spent ten minutes typing variations of *Sorry if that was a weird experience*, but decided I was going to play it cool and not mention our afternoon encounter. Several hours passed with no response. I figured I should forget about it and just enjoy the free bed that came with a limited time offer of sex.

But at three A.M., a response did come: *Bring the money to my house tomorrow at four. We'll be alone.*

# THE STUFFED TURKEY

Jan Vander Laenen

*Avisodomy is the ancient practice of having sex with a bird. As the man is about to orgasm he breaks the neck of the bird causing the bird's cloaca sphincter to constrict and spasm, thus creating pleasurable sensations for the man. [...]Parisian brothels provided turkeys for their clients.*

—B. Love, *The Encyclopaedia of Unusual Sex Practices*

Frédéric, aged around thirty-five, is probably the richest gay man in the small Brussels homosexual ghetto, or at any rate, the gay man with the richest father—a genuine ennobled industrialist—but apparently that does not make him happier; quite the contrary. It would seem that all the sadness on Earth can be read in his beautiful hazel eyes. And yes, those beautiful hazel eyes are not the only winning asset of his appearance. No, no...Frédéric, although somewhat soft, is a distinguished handsome man, slim, with a regular face and neatly trimmed hair, eyebrows, and goatee, and apparently enough hair on his chest to warrant opening the top buttons of his shirt. Furthermore, he is always smartly dressed, jeans of the most fashionable cut, colorful checkered shirts and probably a wardrobe full of jackets in leather, suede, and denim.

And what makes him sad in spite of all this? To put it simply, perhaps because he is the first born and bred son, with three younger brothers and sisters, in what could be considered one of the most poisonous types of nests of our free Western Europe: that of a Flemish family of the high bourgeoisie.

And what does that actually entail? Well, let us say that Frédéric's parents are a spitting image of the bourgeois couple in *La Cage aux Folles*, bearing in mind, however, that that they are still Flemish, not the people with the keenest sense of humor, and that they would not be able to grasp the comic notes of the aforementioned film.

Frédéric does not in the least fit the expectations that his distinguished parents have—or have had—of him. That is to say, he was expected to undertake serious studies at university, such as economics or law, but as he is not exactly the studious type, he wound up earning a diploma in secretaryship and languages, usually reserved for girls. He was actually expected to pursue a solid career among politicians, industrialists and bankers, but because he is more of a dreamer, he is satisfied with a position in one ministry or another that his father found for him. He should have done up a barn of a villa in one of the more elegant suburbs of Brussels, with swimming pool and tennis court, but because he is a rather seedy character, he opted for the center of Brussels, and is all too pleased to live in his father's charming apartment, one of the latter's many properties, on the trendy Rue Dansaert. And above all, he should have long ago entered holy matrimony with the money-mad daughter of another bourgeois, a surgeon or pharmacist or notary, and should have impregnated her at least twice, but he has postponed the exploration of a female body for the time being...just like his coming out, for that matter...

Which has naturally not prevented him from living it up in the gay circuit of Brussels for some eight years, going to most gay bars and cafés in our capital, which are ever so discreet, especially the facades. Furthermore, the aforementioned circuit is so closed in on itself that the chance of rumors about escapades there reaching the ears of his father or someone in his circle is really very small.

Frédéric! On 29 December of last year, it had certainly been some three years since I had a real conversation with him, because for three years I have had a satisfying liaison with another man, and thus had tended to neglect the gay circles of Brussels; but when I think back to Frédéric, it is not without a touch of nostalgia.

And which venues did he grace with his presence in my time? Oh, in addition to the late-hour leather bar Le Duquesnoy and the gay bar Homo Erectus, he was reported often, after working hours, in the Café La Réserve, where he sipped his democratic beer with other gay employees who had left their office in the city center. Incidentally, he was rather out of place there among all these representatives of the "ordinary people." Yes, he could laugh with their "vulgar chatter," but I have never heard him utter ordinary words. Yes, he could participate in a discussion on how, for instance, everything had become more expensive since the introduction of the euro, but his thoughts must have then gone to the series of credit cards in his designer wallet. And yes, he was often courted, especially by bums and what are known as sloshers—but deep down he must have wondered why he was attracting all that attention.

And did he dare take the initiative himself now and then? Well, like everyone else, he flirted now and then, but I am not curious about the erotic lives of others, so I never heard rumors about his tastes or performances, for instance. The fact is that he had made advances to me on several occasions until three years ago, perhaps because he had heard that, as a notary's son, I came somewhat from the same milieu as himself, perhaps a few rungs lower, those rungs between the nobility and the *nouveaux riches*, and was thus supposed to understand his little existential problem.

And indeed, one of the first questions that he asked was whether my family knew of me being otherwise inclined.

"Frédéric!" I cried out, "in our higher Flemish circles, it is not a matter of whether the family knows, but of whether they want to know and how prepared you are yourself to keep it hidden in their circles. No, I lost my virginity—very willingly, for that matter—when I was eighteen, and since then I have made no secret for anyone. When I was twenty-three, I presented my thirteen-year-older Italian friend to my parents, and even told them that we slept in the same bed. In all these years I have run the gamut from queer to transvestite to leather-jacket boy, to fister and fisted, to find myself again as just an ordinary man, but it is only when I started to talk openly about my homosexuality in my stories and to express my doubts about the respectability of the Flemish bourgeois mentality, that the real problems arose. So..."

"You obviously do not like to talk about it," he replied, for he must have noted my relative stiffness, "but what would you advise me in concrete terms?"

"Well, I have broken all family ties. I could perhaps give you the address of my psychiatrist, but I would give you this piece of advice: live your life!"

"What do you mean?"

I got up from our little table in La Réserve and repeated to him the words that an American female friend had sputtered as we were leaving Saint Peter's Basilica in Rome one day: "Let's do something dirty!"

Well, Frédéric and I had never ended up in bed together, and thus I had never done anything dirty with him, nor with that American female friend, for that matter, and as already mentioned, our paths had seldom crossed for some three years. But when I ran into him by chance, I have to admit that he looked radiant somehow...

Ah, that 29 December of last year... I had spent Christmas alone, and it was one of those indefinable days between Christmas and the approaching New Year, a day on which you inertly wait for something that does not come. Fortunately, the weather was mild and sunny, and around three in the afternoon, I went to have a look at the Christmas market on the Place Sainte-Cathérine, where I had a sandwich with German sausage and mustard. And as I was standing at a stall, a wooden shed with wooden counters where Glühwein was served, I bumped into Frédéric.

"Ah, Jan, is everything okay?"

"This Christmas period gets to me in a way," I complained.

"Haven't done anything dirty?"

I looked at him puzzled, whereupon he bid me to take a seat at a small table to drink a glass of warm wine.

"Do you still remember how three years ago, you saw me coming out, together with my parents, of the snobbish restaurant Belga Queen, and you subsequently told me that my mother and father reminded you of that bourgeois couple in *La Cage aux Folles*?

"Yes."

"Well, on Christmas Eve, I found myself in a situation so hilarious as to rival some of the scenes from that film."

"Do tell!"

"A couple of days before Christmas, my mother phoned me at the office, essentially to order me to go and collect the turkey for the Christmas dinner at our estate in La Roche-en-Ardenne, and gave me the mobile phone number of the game warden. So, I got in my car, and after driving for an hour, I arrived at our property, proceeded through the park to the eighteenth-century pavilions, and parked by the hut next to the lower court.

"I knocked but there was no answer, so I went in the hut, saw that the turkey was hanging nicely on a hook among pheasants and rabbits, and just as I was about to dial the number on my mobile, my eye fell on a number of books on a shelf. No, no copy of the Bible or manuals on how to raise rabbits or geese, for instance, but a real list of rather, ahem, erotic works: *Justine* and *Les 120 Jours de Sodom*, by Marquis de Sade, *Adieu à Berlin* by Christopher Isherwood, *Contes Immoraux* by the Prince de Ligne…"

"…and, perhaps, not *L'amant de Lady Chatterley* by Lawrence?" I interrupted.

"Yes, yes…and just when I somewhat curiously started leafing through the books, I heard a reverberating voice behind me: 'And what do you think you are doing?' "

"Mellors?"

"Our game warden, in any event, not Lawrence's, and yes he did look a bit like the actor Nicholas Clay in the filmed version, filthy rubber boots, overalls open at the top showing the hair on his chest, and a frank, unshaven gob. 'I am the baron's son,'

I told him apologetically. 'I have come to collect our turkey for Christmas.' And the scoundrel stepped right up and took me by the chin with his filthy paw of a hand.

" 'What a nice, neat son that rich miser of a baron has, and what nice teeth you have. You see, I'm used to doing this for my job. I always look a horse in the mouth first,' he said to me.

"I smelled on his breath that he had probably already hit the eau de vie.

" 'And you were sniffing about in my book collection, were you?' he asked of me. I was somewhat cornered.

" 'Ah, there is so little to do here in the country, but since I have good taste, I prefer a good wank with an erotic story rather than with porno. You also have a nice snout, a little bit like a greenhouse plant, but...' And he plunged his tongue in my mouth. 'A man or a woman, it makes little difference to me, provided I get my pleasure!' "

"And did you give him his pleasure?" I asked Frédéric.

Frédéric turned red.

"Making love in nature, or in this case, in a hut, has always been one of my favorite fantasies," he said.

"You are preaching to the converted...how I have frisked about in the *pineta* of Viareggio."

"Our Mellors was apparently not averse to French-kissing another man, and he even stuck the tip of his tongue in one of my nostrils, but then I got down to serious business, sucking merrily on his thick nipples, and then gave his member a well-deserved oral treatment."

"You are circumcised?" I asked lecherously, picturing his parts as well.

"My penis was already so thick when I was twelve that they had to operate on me because of foreskin stenosis."

"And...?" I asked.

"Well," he replied, "Later he unbuttoned my trousers and turned me over, but before getting that mushroom and its entire stem to disappear in that spot which is forbidden territory in nearly all religions, he crouched behind me and...well, relaxed my sphincter with his tongue. He moistened it so well with spittle, and gave it such a good rim job, that the skin round my arsehole is still somewhat irritated from the stubbles on his chin."

"And then..."

"And then, in fact, apart from a vigorous thrust, he was as vigorous verbally. Because, 'Yeah, my little daddy's boy,' he began to growl, 'you are giving me as much pleasure as that turkey yesterday. See it hanging there, that poor beast...Oh, what a dignified end did I give it. I first put its dumb head in the drawer of that cupboard, and then stuffed it nice, in and out, in and out, in and out, and when I felt I was about to shoot my load, I slammed the drawer, breaking its neck, and wow...how its poor sphincter constricted round my exploding stick...It was grand, just as described in the handbooks...I scored five erotic capers in one yesterday: sodomy, zoophilia, homosexuality—yes, yes, our turkey is a he, necrophilia and sadism...You needn't worry...I am not going to harm a single hair of our daddy's boy, but I am going to stuff you nicely like your Christmas dinner there....'"

I took a gulp of my Glühwein and looked at Frédéric, somewhat dumbfounded. "And then, he shot his load in your rectum?"

"No, no, he pulled out, ordered me to turn around, kneel down and open my mouth, because it was a sin to spill his valuable seed in a man's hole that has no taste buds."

"You are careful...?" I carefully interrupted my question.

"He reassured me that he was in perfect health and handed me his bottle of eau de vie to rinse out my sticky mouth."

"Wild." I shrugged somewhat indifferently, as I sat with a swollen member in my trousers against the wooden table.

"And dirty, indeed," said Frédéric, concluding his story about his fling with his "Mellors."

"And Christmas Eve?"

"Endless boredom, wouldn't you know, a family dinner in our Art Nouveau manorial house here in Brussels, valets, crystal, porcelain, caviar, foie gras..."

"And stuffed turkey."

"Yes, and when my father said that the turkey was really delicious, and my mother, with her snobbish whistling voice, added that the filling in particular was really juicy, I burst out laughing."

"And did you own up?"

"I was just about to, yes!"

I looked at Frédéric with amusement. "I can truly imagine how such a scene would unfold," I said. "First shocked looks, looks of disbelief, but when you persist that you are not lying, then all mayhem breaks loose in your family. Everyone has to be taken to the hospital there and then to have their stomach pumped, then despair when a doctor tells you that infection with the AIDS virus is detectable in the blood only after three months. 'Mellors,' who would be subjected to a medical test immediately, would naturally be given the sack, and very certainly dragged before a court for gruesome crimes and downright mistreatment of animals, et cetera, et cetera."

"Yes," Frédéric interrupted me. "It is because of that I kept my mouth shut. And when my mother insisted on why I had burst out laughing, I could only reply that I found *juicy* such a juicy word."

"And the evening continued its ordinary course?"

"Yes," Frédéric said with a wink.

And did this story really happen? Oh, yes, just like that poor turkey, may someone break my neck if I have lied. Frédéric and I said good-bye to each other later, and I suppose that he, like a Lady Chatterley in heat, often jaunts down to the family estate in La Roche-en-Ardenne, for extra stuffing.

# ABOUT THE AUTHORS

**SHANE ALLISON** is the author of seven chapbooks, most recently *I Want to Eat Chinese Food Off Your Ass*. He is the editor of *Backdraft* and *Hot Cops*, and his writing has appeared in *Spork*, *Cause and Effect*, *monkey bicycle*, *Mississippi Review*, *Best Black Gay Erotica*, *Best Gay Erotica* and *Ultimate Gay Erotica*. His first poetry collection, *Slut Machine*, is forthcoming from Rebel Satori Press.

**TOMMY LEE "DOC" BOGGS**, after a spell as an inmate of San Quentin, is now a medium-custody prisoner at California's Sierra Corrections Center, serving out a seven-and-a-half year sentence for auto theft and burglary.

**RACHEL KRAMER BUSSEL** (rachelkramerbussel.com) has edited more than twenty-five anthologies, including *Spanked*, *Tasting Him*, *The Mile High Club*, and *Best Sex Writing 2008*, *2009* and *2010*. Her stories appear in *Where the Boys Are*, *Quickies 3*, and *Dorm Porn*, among others. She hosts the In the Flesh Reading Series in New York.

**HANK FENWICK** grew up in the Midwest, but not a lot, and was educated, quite thoroughly, in Chicago. Since then he has lived by pen and wits in New York, Los Angeles, and cities in between. "Holiday from Love" is from a work in progress, not too tentatively titled *Moments of Passion*.

**JAMIE FREEMAN** always dreamed of being in the Ziegfeld Follies, but was born too late and with too little talent. He went to college in Washington, D.C., and eventually became a writer. The rest is history. He can be reached at jamiefreeman2@gmail.com.

**JIMMY HAMADA** lives, loves and learns in New York City. He experiments with blending reality and fiction, as if there's a difference. The story "fifteen minutes nude" is based on an actual session with a famous New York photographer.

**TREBOR HEALEY** (treborhealey.com) is the author of *Through It Came Bright Colors*, *Sweet Son of Pan* and *A Perfect Scar & Other Stories*. He coedited *Queer & Catholic* and contributed to *Best Gay Erotica 2003, 2004, 2006*, and *Best of Best Gay Erotica 2* and *Best American Erotica 2007*.

**RICHARD HENNEBERT** was born in France but now lives in England, with his husband of fourteen years, Alan B. He teaches French and writes short stories.

**DAVID HOLLY,** writing balls out, has produced more cock-gripping stories and bubbly romances than you can shake your booty at. For a genuine tingle in your asshole, check out his complete bibliography at www.gaywriter.org.

**JONATHAN KEMP** is a British writer and academic who teaches gender studies, creative writing (drama and fiction), and literature, as well as being a DJ. His first novel, *London Triptych*, will be published in 2010.

**JAN VANDER LAENEN** lives in Brussels, where he works as an art historian and translator. He is the author of eight collections of short stories, plays, and screenplays, and he has contributed to *Bears* and *Best Gay Love Stories 2009*. He credits Karen Blixen and Edgar Allan Poe as his literary influences.

**JEFF MANN** has published two books of poetry, *Bones Washed with Wine* and *On the Tongue*; a collection of memoir and poetry, *Loving Mountains, Loving Men*; a book of essays, *Edge*; and a volume of short fiction, *A History of Barbed Wire*, winner of a Lambda Literary Award.

**DAVID MAY** contributed to *Drummer* and other gay skin magazines in the 1980s, published two classic story collections in the 1990s, including *Madrugada: A Cycle of Erotic Fictions*, reprinted in 2009 by Nazca Plains, and has contributed to many anthologies, including *Flesh & the Word 3* and *Best Gay Erotica 2007*. He lives in Seattle.

**ROBERT PATRICK** wrote the plays *Kennedy's Children*, *Untold Decades*, *T-Shirts*, and too many others, and the novel *Temple Slave*. He was a participant at the first Off-Off Broadway theater and cradle of gay theater, the Caffe Cino (New York 1958-1968) and maintains a huge website of Cino images at caffecino.wordpress.com.

**SIMON SHEPPARD** (simonsheppard.com) is making his sixteenth appearance in the *Best Gay Erotica* series. He edited the Lambda Award–winning *Homosex: Sixty Years of Gay Erotica* and *Leathermen,* and wrote *In Deep: Erotic Stories; Kinkorama; Sex Parties 101* and *Hotter Than Hell.* His work has also appeared in nearly three hundred anthologies.

**NATTY SOLTESZ** (bacteriaburger.com) has had stories published in *Best Gay Erotica 2009*, *Second Person Queer*, and *Best Gay Romance 2009*, regularly publishes fiction in *Freshmen*, *Mandate*, and *Handjobs,* is a faithful contributor to the Nifty Erotic Stories Archive, and is writing his first novel, *Backwoods*. He lives in Pittsburgh with his lover.

**THOM WOLF** (myspace.com/thomwolfspace) has published two erotic novels, *Words Made Flesh* and *The Chain*; his short stories have appeared in numerous anthologies and magazines. He lives with his husband Liam in England, where he is a student of creative writing and continues to dabble with gay porn.

**ROB WOLFSHAM** is a twenty-three-year-old token living in Lubbock fucking Texas. His work appears in *Boy Crazy* and *College Boys*, from Cleis Press, and *I Like It Like That: True Tales of Gay Desire*, from Arsenal Pulp Press. He writes for the gayzine Nightcharm.com. Eat his blog at wolfshammy.com.

# ABOUT THE EDITORS

**RICHARD LABONTÉ** has been series editor of *Best Gay Erotica* since 1997, and won the Lambda Literary Award for best gay erotica in 2005 (with judge William Mann) and 2009 (with judge James Lear). Another Lammy came his way in 2007 for *First Person Queer* (Arsenal Pulp Press), coedited with Lawrence Schimel. He has edited a couple of dozen anthologies for Cleis Press, coedited four for Arsenal Pulp, writes book reviews (queer and otherwise) and edits technical writing. He lives on a small, friendly island off the coast of Vancouver, British Columbia, with his husband Asa and a couple of dogs who live to chase deer. Contact: tattyhill@gmail.com.

**BLAIR MASTBAUM** is the author of *Clay's Way* and *Us Ones In Between* and the coeditor of *Cool Thing: Best Gay Fiction from Young American Writers*. He lives in Portland, Oregon, just a mile from important Lewis and Clark historical sites.